Aegolius Creek

Aegolius Creek

Micah Thorp

This is a work of fiction. Names, characters, places, and incidents either are the product of the author's imagination or are used fictitiously. Any resemblance to actual persons, living or dead, events, or locales is entirely coincidental.

Copyright © 2025 by Micah Thorp

All rights reserved. No part of this book may be reproduced or used in any manner without written permission of the copyright owner except for the use of quotations in critical articles and book reviews.

Library of Congress Cataloging-in-Publication Data

Names: Thorp, Micah, 1969– , author.
Title: Aegolius Creek / Micah Thorp.
Description: 190 pages. – First edition. | Laguna Hills, California: Type Eighteen Books, 2025.
Summary: "After a new species of vole is discovered in Don Karlsson's trees, he must protect his homestead, his family, and his livelihood in a courtroom fight that engulfs his community and spills over into protests and riots, while dealing with the conflicting interests of his children and their lingering grief after the loss of their mother."— Provided by publisher.
Identifiers: LCCN 2025932255 | ISBN: 9798992040548 (paperback) | ISBN: 9798992040555 (ebook)
LC record available at https://lccn.loc.gov/2025932255

Published by Type Eighteen Books
www.typeeighteenbooks.com

Printed in the United States

For Mom and Dad

PROLOGUE

"The heavens will disappear with a roar; the elements will be destroyed by fire, and the earth and everything done in it will be laid bare."

— 2 PETER 3:10

Everything begins and ends in fire. That's what Mrs. Green told me when I was eleven in her youth Bible study at the Aegolius Creek Community Church. God created the heavens and the earth from a great ball of flame. Which didn't seem much different than the Big Bang Theory, although Mrs. Green said it was blasphemous to suggest something other than God was responsible for creation. She'd obviously never discussed the matter with Mr. Spence at Crawfordsville High School, who later claimed the only way God created anything was with the laws of physics, and this clearly proved the Big Bang had happened. In either case, it doesn't matter who was right, because whomever you believe, everything began with fire.

According to both, it will end the same way. The Bible says God will incinerate everything anyway. And if Mr. Spence's insights into astrophysics are to be believed, it's the same end result. The sun goes nova and burns the earth to a crisp before absorbing its matter and energy. All of which is to say that if fire is the starting point for everything, it's also the end. All matter, all energy, all of creation, it all began with fire. And everything created eventually burns. Even those things that last forever. They all end in flames.

I WOKE up when my head bounced off the wheel well in the back of the truck. Tad had said to get some sleep—not a problem after four days in the bush. Jose was driving, which considering his driving record seemed like a bad idea, along with the decision to run alongside the east side of the mountains instead of crossing over and taking a straight shot up I-5.

We drove through the hole-in-the-wall, one-traffic-light hamlets of Chiloquin, Chemult, and Crescent, pleasant enough even in the back of a dirty, yellow pickup. After crossing over Willamette Pass, we followed Highway 58 down to Oakridge and stopped for a piss break. Whenever Pop took me up the mountains to go fishing, we'd stop here at the A&W or the ice cream shop, get a snack, and head to the restrooms in the back. But that was years ago. After the mill shut down, those places disappeared. Jose stopped at a little park on the way into town that had a couple porta-potties.

Then I jumped back into the bed of the truck and passed out. I'd say I dreamed, but I don't think I did. No one dreams exhausted but if I did, it was of smoke. Dark, thick, deep gray smoke. Which is pretty much like not dreaming at all.

TAD SEEMED surprised when he told us we were moving. The crew was at base camp getting a meal, filling the water truck, and drinking whatever terrible beer had been foisted upon us when we heard him swear several times. Every morning, Tad and the other crew leaders received a report from Central Command, which I've heard is in some boardroom in Salem or Eugene. The report relayed our marching orders—where to go, how long the fire lines were supposed to run, and other stuff. Half the time, we ended up ignoring the orders because Tad would see something the "experts" in command hadn't—standing snags, masses of brush, or another sign no one in Salem looking at satellite photos or weather radar would notice.

Tad had been fighting fires with the Forest Service for almost ten years, about nine years more than the rest of us, so when he told us to do something, we did—even if it was different from the orders handed down by Central Command. Anyone who saw Tad could tell he'd spent years working out of doors. His ruddy face was aged beyond his years, and his thick torso rippled whenever he swung an ax.

Jose bounced up to the truck holding a large sandwich. He never stopped eating—at least, not as I could tell. We could be out digging, running the hose, hacking back brush, or building a line, and Jose did it all with one hand. Tamara said Jose had a metabolic disorder, which made sense given how skinny he was despite the fact he was always snacking on something.

When we gathered, Tad took a minute to guzzle from a bottle of water before he spoke. "Looks like we're movin' out," he said.

Tamara groaned as she flipped her dirty blonde ponytail from one side of her neck to the other. "I was getting used to this place." She shook her head. "We don't have this one under control. Why are we moving?"

Tad shrugged. "No idea. Order didn't say. We're goin' to Age-o-lus Crick." He paused and looked at the yellow slip of paper. "Agg-ole-us Crick." He paused again. "Og-lee-is Crick."

I grabbed the paper from his hand and stared at the block-typed sheet. "Aegolius Creek," I said. "Ay-go-lee-us. I grew up there."

Tad raised an eyebrow. "What the hell kind of name is Aegolius?"

"It's a kind of owl."

Tamara took a swig of beer. "An owl? Never heard of it."

"It's an owl in Europe. I think."

She punched my shoulder. "Chris is from a place named after a European owl. Sounds about right."

They always gave me crap about being in college. It used to bother me. Tinges of self-consciousness and fears of being identified as privileged had gradually given way to acceptance. I was the college kid mixed in with a hardened, blue-collar bunch, the one who used an occasional big word or referenced an obscure name. I was smart but not wise, intelligent but not experienced, clever but green. I'd grown accustomed to the role.

"The kicker is," I said, "that owl is supposed to be an omen of bad luck." As the words left my mouth, I realized it probably wasn't a wise thing to say.

Tad grimaced and Jose turned to walk away.

"Great. We're going to a place named after a bad omen." Tamara punched my shoulder again, harder.

"It's just a name," I said.

WHEN WE TURNED off the freeway and drove up the valley, the curves started to change. The wide, slow arches that traced the edges of Dexter Reservoir became tight turns back and forth along the McKenzie River, and finally, the breaks and bumps up the Aegolius. We passed the shake mill, the fishpond, and the old railroad. About halfway up the valley, Jose pulled over.

Tamara stopped behind us in the water truck. She'd named the vehicle Rudy after an old boyfriend who left her when she joined the Army. Rudy the truck wasn't in the best shape, with balding tires and the Forest Service logo nearly worn off its driver-side door. It was on the smaller side and held about five thousand gallons; a portable pump was attached to the back. We could take that truck nearly anywhere—old logging roads, dried creek beds, washed-out gullies. Every time we needed to douse some charred embers or put out a flag fire, Rudy could get close enough to make it so. I wondered if the real Rudy had been as reliable as Rudy the truck, until he wasn't.

We gathered around the hood of the pickup and Tad pulled out a folded paper. Forest Service maps were an essential tool for navigating the area around a fire. Usually, cell service would be out and GPS spotty. He looked at the coordinates on his phone, stared at the map for a minute, then looked up at the sky.

"Spotters on Butte Tower tagged smoke coming from there." He pointed at the horizon. "But I don't see a whisper."

Jose leaned against the pickup, pulled some kind of candy bar from his pocket, and pointed at me. "Show him. You're from around here."

Tad handed me the map. He put his finger on the coordinates.

It took a moment to orient myself to the curved lines and jagged symbols outlining the contour of the tiny valley. I lived about five miles up the Aegolius Highway from first grade until I left for college. The area at the end of Tad's finger gradually became recognizable. I tapped the spot. "That's the old Karlsson ranch."

He looked up. "Anyone live there?"

I cleared my throat. "Used to be. Old man Karlsson, two boys and a girl. I think the kids have moved away. I'm not sure if anyone's left."

The Karlssons were an odd clan. The three Karlsson kids were all much older than me. Growing up, I hadn't had much interaction with them, and what I knew mostly came from hearsay and gossip. Their homestead lay near the northeastern end of the Aegolius Valley, up where the creek first rolled out of the Cascade foothills. Mrs. Karlsson had died during the birth of her third child, Zeke, and rumor had it the older two kids mostly raised themselves.

Tad sighed and folded up the map. "Here's the deal. We need to get up there, look for structures in the vicinity, and try to protect them. We'll start containment and report back if it looks like we need help. Supposedly, this is a small fire."

Jose, Tamara, and I nodded, knowing "small fire" could be interpreted several different ways.

Then Tad added something we hadn't heard him say before. "Oh, and there's one other thing. Given the dry EMC and the lack of a weather event—" He looked at us. "If you see anyone in the area, don't approach them. Tell me immediately. Anyone."

Tamara looked at Jose and me. "What did he just say?"

Jose shrugged.

"He's suggesting the fire could be man-made." I looked at Tad.

He frowned. "Not just man-made. *Intentionally* man-made."

Jose raised his eyebrows. "You mean like arson?"

Tad didn't respond as he climbed back in the truck.

WE DROVE FURTHER up the valley. The two-lane road became one, and the asphalt gradually turned to gravel. The Aegolius Valley was a mile wide and thirty miles long. Hills covered in Doug fir, oak, pine, and alder lined the narrow valley floor. The road and rail line, both used to haul timber off the hillsides and into nearby mill towns, flanked the meandering creek. The mysterious smoke plume we hadn't seen as we entered the valley gradually became visible as the road narrowed.

It was soon clear why Tad was worried about arson. The valley was still too wet for a fire to start without propellant, and no recent storms meant no lightning strikes. I'd never seen a forest fire started on purpose and wasn't entirely sure what it meant. Why would anyone start a fire near Aegolius Creek?

When we arrived at the base of the smoke plume, the sky reddened, and we saw flames for the first time. Doug Firs, a hundred feet tall, were being shredded by the blaze. Sword fern and dogwood at the base of the great trees smoldered as flames climbed through the canopy. The trees on fire were taller than the rest of the surrounding forest and the tallest were immediately adjacent to the road, giving the illusion of a great basilica awash in flame. Jose drove the truck slowly up the gravel road into the inferno. The road cut through the giant pillars of fire, close enough to redden the skin, distant enough not to burn, as we entered the nave. The pews astride the road were filled with flames, reaching to the heavens like the forlorn hands of sinners seeking to escape perdition.

As we drove on, the intensity of the flames increased. Tad yelled something, but the fire was too loud for the rest of us to hear. Campfires crackle and pop. Brush fires whirl and snap. Forest fires roar.

Somewhere near the center of the fire, I made out a small dwelling about the size of a double-wide trailer. If this was the structure we were expected to protect, I couldn't imagine what we could do to save it. A couple hundred feet away, we hopped out. As Tamara started to pull the hose and pump off Rudy, Jose grabbed a chainsaw from the back of the pickup. But Tad waved us off, signaling that the fire was too hot. We prepared to retreat when Tamara screamed and pointed at the house.

In the midst of the inferno, the silhouette of a man stumbled through the front door, his face obscured by smoke and flames. We yelled to drop and roll and pushed forward before being repelled by the heat. Instead of running from the burning house, a lone figure stood unmoved. From the porch, he yelled something we couldn't make out over the roar of the fire. He raised his fist and made no effort to step off the porch. It was clear he was not leaving. Tad grabbed the pump and tried to roll out the hose, but the fire was moving too fast. As we watched, flames engulfed the man, who, in one final act, extended the middle finger of his clenched hand.

CHAPTER ONE

"I went to the woods because I wanted to live deliberately...and not, when I came to die, discover that I had not lived."

— *HENRY DAVID THOREAU*

WHERE THE SNOWPACKS trickle down the western Cascades into the Santiam, Calapooia, Blue River, and McKenzie—and the alpine forests of mountain hemlock, silver fir, and yellow oak transition to temperate Douglas fir, madrona and bigleaf maple—there sits a decayed, lichen-covered house. A dirty, faded yellow, it blends with the sword fern, blackberry, and poison oak that push up the cinder block foundation onto its aluminum sides. Resting among the trees and ferns as though part of the undergrowth, it rises from the forest floor like toadstools and moss. Sixty-year-old Douglas firs, pillars in an Acropolistic forest, tower over the little house cowering in their midst.

A gravel driveway rolls up to the front porch, which is covered with a corrugated fiberglass roof so densely packed with detritus its translucence is gone. Rotting leaves and needles block what light filters down through the forest canopy, darkening the entrance to the tiny abode. The rays managing to penetrate the maze of branches create an ethereal glow that radiates from the rusted siding along the rotted wooden baseboard attached to the base of the house.

Behind the tiny abode, a pole barn, covered in moss and missing cedar shingles, is surrounded by a pair of rusting tractors, half-buried in brambles. A shallow slope, covered by oak and cedar, rolls from the barn down to Aegolius Creek. The changeable body of water was called a "creek" by pioneers homesteading in the late summer, but it rises and falls throughout the year. In late spring when the snow in the mountains melts and rain pours on the foothills, the Aegolius swells and rises until it nearly reaches the pole barn, with pools deep enough they can't be crossed without a boat. In late summer, it shrinks to a trickle, so small in places a man can jump clear across without a splash. Had the homesteaders found the Aegolius during mid-winter, it might have been named the Aegolius River, but many labels placed on mutable objects reflect only the transient perceptions of those seeing them for the first time.

HARVEY WHITE JOLTS upright as the Lear touches down. He rubs his face and swallows a remaining swig of whiskey. The flight to Portland was shorter than he expected. Twelve hours from Sapporo. Not bad.

His phone wakes and buzzes as the plane taxis toward the terminal. The market's been open for hours. Harvey scrolls through his messages. Mr. Chantois wants to know about movement on the Enstrom merger, someone from Goldman has a question about interest rates, and an investor keeps asking for a new prospectus. Harvey twists the bezel on his watch. It's a silver and black diving watch. He doesn't dive but likes the look—makes him feel less like a pudgy, sun-deprived hedge fund manager.

The jet's door opens, and a few passengers stumble onto the tarmac. Harvey is surprised by the cold.

"Mr. White?" A man wearing a canvas jacket and jeans shoves his hand into Harvey's. "Rob Meyer. RGL land management."

An attendant hands over his briefcase and duffle bag. Rob doesn't offer to carry them, which Harvey notes and appreciates. Not an ass kisser. Tall and lean, with thinning salt and pepper hair, Rob looks every bit the field professional Harvey expected.

Rob motions toward a black, Ford F-150 pickup. "It's about a two-and-a-half-hour ride. If you want to hit the head or grab something to eat, I'd do it now."

Harvey nods. He suddenly feels overdressed in a blazer and Italian loafers. No matter. "I'm fine. I need to leave by six, so let's get moving."

Rain drizzles as the truck makes its way down I-5. The cab of the pickup is more comfortable than Harvey expected. Nice leather seats. And it feels good to sit up high. After thinking for a moment, he realizes he's never been in a pickup. He wonders if there's a dealership near his office in Manhattan.

Harvey makes some calls as the truck rolls from Portland onto the flat grasslands of the Willamette Valley.

Rob looks ahead and pretends not to overhear the conversations Harvey is having next to him.

As Harvey finishes and puts down the phone, Rob clears his throat. "The stand we're going to look at has about 720 acres of forty-year-old Doug Firs. In a decade, we figure there will be about forty million board feet per acre, for a total of—"

"Thirty thousand MBF," Harvey interrupts. "And at today's prices that's around twenty million." It's Harvey's number one rule: always know your numbers. Always.

After an hour and a half, the truck turns off I-5 and onto a two-lane highway headed east, toward the forested foothills at the valley's edge. Rob stops at a run-down Chevron station, and Harvey steps out and stretches. He looks around, trying to get his bearings.

"What's the name of this place?"

"Brownsville."

"Not much to look at."

"Used to be—" Rob points at a dry canal not far from the gas station. "A millrace up there. Large wool mill that eventually moved to Pendleton. And a handful of timber mills in this area as well. The Calapooia River was never big enough for timber rafting, but there were plenty of trees."

Harvey grimaces. "Hard to sell timber without any mills around."

"There're mills enough, but none in these smaller towns." Rob nods toward the road. "At one time, nearly every hamlet and two-traffic-light crossroads west of the Cascades had a mill. Now only a few dozen are left in the whole state."

The two men climb back into the truck. Rob hands Harvey a thermos. "This'll wake you up." Harvey unscrews the top and pours dark black coffee into the metal cup lid. He notes the coffee is the color and consistency of used motor oil.

The truck rolls through Brownsville, then Crawfordsville, and finally turns onto the Aegolius Highway. The grassland valley disappears as the spaces between the tree-covered hills narrow. Despite the density of the forest covering the valley floor, Harvey notices a few dilapidated houses along the hillsides. "I didn't think anyone lived out here."

"There are still a few folks. Mostly retired or never wanted to leave."

They turn off the highway, and a dirt road weaves up a hill on the north side of the valley. The ruts become deeper, and the forest leans into the truck. After an hour of bouncing up and down, the truck rolls into an open space and comes to a halt.

As he steps out of the cab, Harvey gasps at the view. The meadow where the truck has stopped is flat, about the size of a basketball court, and below is the entire expanse of the valley. The Aegolius forest stretches out like a giant, green quilt, folded in half with a creek and highway running like silver and blue threads up the middle. Little squares of trees—fir, hemlock, and pine interspersed with the occasional maple and cedar—dot the hillsides. He takes a breath, smells the green, and inhales the cool, damp clean. Briefly, he wonders why anyone would consider cutting any of it down.

Rob walks to the edge of the meadow and pulls a map from his back pocket. "This is an old landing site for a logging operation." He points. "We're here." He nods across the valley. "The acreage is there."

Harvey motions to the hills on the other side of the valley. "Why are those trees smaller than the ones next to them?"

"Everything in this forest has been logged and replanted at least once over the last century. Each stand was planted at a different time. That's one of the younger ones."

He nods. "I get it. It's like fields in the Midwest. One square is soybeans, the next is corn, and the next is wheat. It's not a forest; it's a farm."

Rob points toward the north end of the valley. "Some of the land is owned by Forest Service, and the feds aren't allowing harvesting any time soon. However, we've identified several large plots that are privately owned. We've approached several landowners. Most are open to selling, but a couple are dug in."

Harvey squints. He looks across the breadth of the valley, estimating the size and value of each stand, wondering which can be acquired and eventually cut. His eyes work their way along the hillsides. "What about those?" He points toward a section of the forest in the northeastern corner of the valley. The trees look enormous compared to the rest of the surrounding forest, plainly visible to the naked eye from this distance, miles away. Their darkened hue rises at least twenty feet above the rest of the forest canopy.

Rob looks at the trees and back at the map. "It's an old homestead. There are a few of those left. Owner likely planted it fifty or sixty years ago."

Harvey's eyebrows rise. "Seriously? None of the shacks we passed coming up here look like they belong to landowners."

"Oh, I'd bet most do. Most own at least a couple acres."

Harvey scratches his head. "There's a lot of timber around those homes. You'd think they'd sell and buy a decent house. Those trees are probably worth a lot."

Rob folds the map up. "Lotta folks around here are timber rich and cash poor. It's just how it is. Folks'll live in a one-room shack with a million dollars worth of trees, and they don't ever intend to cut."

Rob points at an area near the valley floor, where a stand of smaller trees is next to larger ones. "See there. You can tell those trees are private. Not on federal BLM land. Someone cut whatever was there back in the '80s and replanted, probably because of the spotted owl."

Harvey squints. "You mean they cut the trees on their land?"

Rob nods. "Yup. People thought they might never have a chance to cut them again. So, they cut everything. After the spotted owl was listed as endangered, there was more loggin' and cuttin'—at least, for a while."

Harvey notices a house across the valley. A single-wide trailer stuck amid a grove of madronas and firs. "Why don't they cut them now? That guy over there probably has enough trees to buy a new house, or maybe two."

"As long as they know the trees are worth something, and

they can log whenever they want, there isn't a pissin' chance they'd cut 'em."

Harvey shakes his head in disbelief. "Why?"

Rob smiles. "People aren't afraid of being poor. What they fear is not having the chance to be rich."

In 1903, when Elias Karlsson forged his way up the Aegolius to stake his claim, he wasn't certain where the property borders started and ended. An insatiable drive for permanence—something not afforded the Karlsson clan in the crowded slums of the Atlantic seaboard or across the landlocked Midwest—pushed Elias further and further west, all the way to the edge of the Pacific, where a man could live on a parcel for only three years before calling it his own.

Unlike his siblings, Elias could read. He found a General Land Office brochure of the Western Cascades in a garbage bin behind his tenement with the words "free land" and a description of beautiful mountains and lush forests. The next day, with a few dollars and the clothes on his back, he jumped a train and headed west. Upon arrival in Oregon, penniless and starving, he was taken in by the owner of a livery who gave him room and board in exchange for cleaning stalls. A few weeks later, he made his way to the federal building in Salem, where he was given papers and a map. The map was a checkerboard of little squares representing plots of 160 acres. Only one square had a ribbon of water running through it. Karlsson couldn't pronounce Aegolius, but he knew land with water was more valuable than land without, so he scratched his initials on the deed, borrowed an old mare from the livery, and rode out to find his lot.

Elias's map didn't include several twists and turns in the Aegolius and when he stopped for the night, he wasn't sure whether he was close to his land or not. After a few days wandering up and down the creek bed, he decided that one particular bend marked the edge of his claim. An hour later he found a grove of trees, and a clearing with room for a small house, and a trail that might be wide enough for a wagon to make its way up from the valley floor.

Concerned he might not be able to find the claim when he returned, Elias determined to create a distinct marker near the creek. For several hours, he hauled river rock from the creek bed to the northeast corner of the lot. Despite limited schooling, he'd been fascinated by pictures of Egypt, so he shaped the stone pile into a pyramid, with a rectangular base, evenly sloped sides, and a perfect peak. When complete, it stood nearly six feet high.

A month later, he was back with a bull saw, an ax, and a team. By the time the fall rains came, he had carved space for a cabin and barn. A latrine sat downwind from the cabin, and a fence around the parcel of land was under construction. By the following winter, the entire homestead—based on Karlsson's best estimation of property lines—had been fenced, and the cabin had grown into a small house. Two years after he started building, a pole barn was erected, and a pair of cows wandered around a nearby open meadow.

Elias's next addition was a bit more difficult to obtain than the pole barn or fence. Friday trips to Crawfordsville, Sweet Home, and Albany led to invitations from various church groups, dance halls, and social clubs. The awkward, bearded landowner with a quick wit and somewhat uncouth behavior incurred interest from several different families within the small communities; they made certain their daughters were present whenever he was around. Most of the young women showed initial interest, until they visited his spartan homestead. In time, Wilma Turner, a sturdy twenty-year-old with an abusive father, decided her fate with Elias was better than remaining at home on a sheep farm near Albany. After a brief courtship, the two were wed, and she moved into Elias's humble abode.

Despite her youth, Wilma Karlsson proved hearty enough for the homestead, bearing three daughters and two sons—one who died at birth—all the while taking care of a small flock of sheep, two cows, and a small garden. As the children grew, the Karlsson household flourished. By the time the Great War ended, the cabin had grown to several rooms, and the wagon had been replaced with a tractor.

Elias worked for Graham's Timber, a small logging outfit that cut trees on the Forest Service land adjacent to the homestead. When no one needed roughshod fir coming from the mill in Sweet Home, the family lived off livestock and the forest around the tiny house. Elias hunted elk, deer, and grouse, while Wilma sold eggs and wool to a cooperative in Brownsville.

By the middle of the Roaring '20s, Elias decided it was time to sell all the timber on his land. That same year, the boy, Timothy, left home and made his way to Seattle, where he worked on a merchant ship. After a few years, he returned on leave to find nearly every tree on the homestead cut and a new Ford Model T sitting on the dirt road leading to the house.

As the decade ended, the farm flourished with a small herd of cattle and a dozen or so sheep. While Elias worked at the sawmill in Crawfordsville, Wilma and her three daughters managed the farm. The older girls, Margaret and Kathy, were regularly courted by young men making their way up the dirt road to buy a dozen eggs or to offer a hand chopping wood. The youngest daughter, Helen, attended the newly built Aegolius Creek Primary School.

But good fortune didn't last long for the Karlssons. Three years after the stock market crashed, Elias became ill and couldn't farm the land as he once had. Timothy, returning home after an injury at sea, didn't have the strength to step in.

Then, in 1932, Elias died while repairing a fence on the northwest corner of the property. Wilma tried to keep the farm running, but when the oldest daughter, Kathy, married and left for Oregon City, she and the other two other girls, Helen and Margaret, moved back into town, leaving Timothy alone.

Timothy Karlsson didn't last long on the homestead. Listless and haunted, he struggled to maintain the house, flock, and cows. He began to drink. Soon, the house fell into disrepair, the animals either disappeared or died, and there was nothing more of value to sell. He tried to sell the land, but during the depression there were no buyers. Finally, penniless, Timothy left the homestead and was never seen again.

HARVEY NOTICES the ride back down the hillside feels less bumpy than the way up. He is quiet, contemplative. As the truck turns onto Aegolius Highway, he says, "I wonder what investors would do if they saw this place."

Rob rolls down his window and spits out another wad. "What do you mean?"

"Would they suddenly feel like the people who own the trees—not wanting to cut them down unless they're forced?" Harvey points to the hillsides. "It's beautiful and green. I'm sure at some level, people see this as something to preserve."

"I suppose."

Harvey looks at another tiny, run-down house. "Why didn't everyone leave when the mills shut down? Their livelihoods weren't going to come back."

"They just keep hangin' on. People do what they know. And even when circumstances change, they keep doin' what they did before, hoping it's all going to be the same."

Rob points at a field with a large mound of dirt in the middle. "See that over there? That's the edge of a big crater. Hole in the middle goes down about ten feet. Belonged to a guy named Russ Mooney. Russ was a logger, old-school kind of guy. Lived in a trailer with a woman and two kids. The crummy would stop right next to it and pick him up with his—"

Harvey holds up his hand. "What? What would pick him up?"

"A crummy. These dirty old school buses would take the loggers up to the site. Back in the day, you'd see them running up and down in the morning and evening. Taking guys to work in the woods and bringin' 'em back at night." Rob spits another wad out the window before continuing.

"Anyway, Russ was a hardheaded logger. His dad and uncles were loggers. Only thing they knew was the woods. They were born here, died here. Had sawdust in their veins. Several years ago, Russ tried to remove a stump that was out in the middle of that field. It was an old, white oak that had snapped in half during a windstorm. Russ wanted to remove the whole tree, roots and all. He ground the stump down to the ground and then dug some holes underneath what was left and threw a few sticks of dynamite in. Blew the hell out of that thing. Afterwards, some big roots were still buried in the crater he'd created, so he dug holes around the roots and stuck some more dynamite in and blew the hell out of the roots.

"When he was done the crater was deeper, but there were still roots in the bottom of it. He tried again to dig them out but couldn't, so he blew 'em up again." Rob chuckles. "What he didn't realize is that white oaks have some of the deepest roots in nature. They root down deep in the place where they grow. And trying to move them—well, you'll never dig that deep. In the end, what was left was a big hole in the ground, and the roots of the tree were still buried beneath it."

. . .

It was Helen's son Donald who decided to return to the Karlsson homestead in 1955. Elias' death and Timothy's disappearance had left the remaining Karlsson clan scattered across the small towns dotting the Willamette Valley. In the aftermath of her father's death, Helen married and had a son and daughter before sending her husband away and reclaiming the Karlsson name.

Helen had decided the Aegolius Valley was cursed, along with anyone who might wish to live there. Haunted by the loss of her father and brother, she proclaimed to her children that waters of the Aegolius were laced with poison, and the lands around the old house were barren and fallow.

A precocious and independent child, Donald spent most of his childhood doing precisely whatever he was told not to do. He managed to remain in school until the eighth grade, at which point he decided he didn't require any more book learning. Able to live off the land, he would frequently take his horse and his 30-06 Springfield and disappear into the Coburg Hills for days at a time. Recognizable by the coonskin cap he wore into his twenties, he could be seen from Highway 99, marching across sheep fields and through cornrows. Occasionally a farmer might find the carcass of a coyote or a pile of dead nutria outside their barn, a sign Donald had recently been there.

Helen's exhortations and admonitions about the Aegolius homestead engendered enough curiosity to ensure the wayward Donald would eventually find his way there. After a day following the meandering creek, he located the shell of the old house. Land that had been cleared when the house was abandoned by Timothy was now dotted with eye-high Doug firs and the occasional waist-high alder or cedar.

Initially he wasn't sure where to look, but the river rock pyramid, created by Elias and still a part of Karlsson family lore, assured Donald he had arrived. Driving his horse further up the creek, he saw the outlines of the original Karlsson home.

The house was dilapidated and falling apart. Nearly half of the cedar shingles on the roof were gone. The porch was in a general state of collapse, and grass grew through the planks. The front door hung by a single hinge.

Whatever Donald might have lacked in civility, he made up for in fortitude. Perhaps he felt a sense of debt left by his forebearers, or the ghost of Elias had settled within his grandson. In either case, he immediately felt the urge to plant his roots deep into the clay along the creek.

Donald began work as a choker setter for Crawfordsville Forest Products, running up and down hillsides rolling cables around the midsection of felled trees, which were then pulled uphill to a landing site. It was hard, dirty, and dangerous work he did several days a month. The rest of the time, he worked on the homestead, building and rebuilding the structure Elias had erected three decades prior. He bought a used truck, and after a year, the dirt road to his rebuilt house was covered with gravel.

By the mid-1960s, Donald decided it was time to marry. Like his grandfather, he began to frequent the local church, the grange, and occasionally, the dance hall. Marlene Rayburn, a petite eighteen-year-old, sat next to him at a church potluck where at first, he barely noticed her. But after she reached across the table in an unnecessary gesture designed to garner his attention, he couldn't help but see. The young Don was immediately taken by her black hair, bright blue eyes, and infectious laugh. Over the next hour, he barely spoke as she captivated him with her quick wit and charming demeanor.

Marlene's father owned the only gas station in Crawfordsville and kept that monopoly by virtue of a seat on the town council. Though stern, he adored his daughters, who in turn prized the special relationship they shared with their father. Since his station was the only source for gas or propane within thirty miles, every farmer, rancher, and homesteader was careful not to cross him. It was thus, with some trepidation, that Donald decided to talk to Marlene's father.

For weeks, Donald could think of little other than Marlene. Finally, he drove to the filling station one afternoon and asked to see the owner.

Marlene's father was impressed that the young man had the courtesy to ask permission to call on his daughter. He knew little of him, other than he owned land up the Aegolius. Fortunately for Donald, little else mattered in the station owner's mind, for owning land was a sign of either fortitude or tenacity, traits he regarded as necessities for success. A firm handshake sealed the impression, and Donald set out at once to call on Marlene.

Self-conscious about his unrefined appearance and inarticulate conversational skills, Donald mostly listened, and Marlene mostly talked. Her narratives enthralled him. She talked about her family and friends, and about the books she had read and the movies she had seen. It was as though she had a never-ending series of tales to impart, and he had an infinite capacity to receive them. Perhaps it was the many years he had spent living alone in the woods, or maybe it was Marlene's piercing blue eyes. Whatever the reason, he knew from the beginning of their courtship he didn't want to live his life without her. Within a few short months, Donald asked again for permission—this time to marry her.

It was a simple wedding at the Brownsville Community Church. Business had declined at the filling station, and Marlene's father wouldn't spend more than necessary to see his youngest daughter wed.

Life on the homestead was harder than Marlene had anticipated. Donald had made the house habitable but had invested little in comfort. Almost immediately, she began to procure furniture, linens, silverware, and all the other necessities needed to turn the spartan house into a home. An old rug from her mother, a set of dishes from a friend at church, a basket from one of the boys at the gas station—Marlene was a bird bringing twigs and lint back to the nest. Donald, wise enough to stand by, simply smiled and nodded approvingly at whatever new addition she made to the household.

By the late 1960s, Donald had steady work at the Crawfordsville mill, and Marlene had a fully furnished home, a large garden, and pastured cows.

It was during these idyllic days that Donald Karlsson decided to plant some trees.

Donald's trees weren't anything special. Just regular old Doug firs. The same trees that grew up and down the western slope of the Cascades, across the Willamette Valley and onto the Coast Range. The same trees that had been logged, planted, logged, planted, and logged again. The same trees that were cut into thirty-two-foot lengths, hauled up to a landing platform on a choker cable, limbed, yarded, and hauled. The same trees that were milled into two-by-fours, four-by-fours, and four-by-eights, put on trains and trucks, distributed to lumberyards, and pounded into the shapes of houses by an army of framers, carpenters, and roofers. Donald's trees were no different.

One morning, he hauled a truckload of seedlings up the dirt road. He estimated that one in ten would survive, and at four hundred seedlings per acre, he'd need roughly ten thousand to cover the meadow that was left when his grandfather logged the homestead after the Great War. A foreman at the mill in Springfield had shown him how to drive the hazel hoe into the ground, pry open the soil, drop the seedlings in, and stomp the ground back into place. In normal replantings, the process was carried over and over thousands of times. It all seemed rough, industrialized.

Donald decided if he used a more nurturing approach, it might increase the growth of the trees. Carefully, he planted each tree a few feet apart. He cut the weeds and grass around each seedling. In a large can, he beat cayenne pepper, eggs, milk, powdered soap, and oil, which he sprinkled around the base of each tiny tree to keep the deer away.

While Donald attempted to grow trees, Marlene sought to grow a family. By the early 1970s, after years of being chided by women at church and her father, Marlene told her husband they were going to have a baby. Donald assumed her declaration was strictly in the future tense, until Marlene requested a bassinette, a rocker, and some cotton flannel for diapers.

On July 2, 1972, Marlene Karlsson gave birth to William Elias Karlsson. Delivered in the early hours of the morning, he entered the world with a bellowing cry and a shock of jet-black hair. Marlene's mother and sisters were in attendance. Donald was not.

HARVEY REMAINS quiet while the F-150 rolls through Crawfordsville. When they reach I-5, he taps a finger on the dashboard. "You know what I love about the timber business?"

Rob shakes his head.

"Trees grow."

Rob gives him a quizzical look.

Harvey clears his throat. "Most investments grow over time. They go up a little, then down a little, but gradually, they increase in value. But the actual thing you invest in doesn't really change. If I buy an auto factory, the factory doesn't change much. It may become more valuable as cars become more expensive, but the buildings or what they produce do not change. Unlike a factory, trees grow. Doesn't matter whether the value goes up or down—the physical trees grow. I figure, as an investment, the real value of the trees themselves grows between five and ten percent a year. There aren't many other investments with that kind of guaranteed return."

Rob nods. "Does that mean you're interested?"

Harvey smiles. "I'm always interested."

"Well, we can certainly help negotiate the purchase. Getting some of these folks to sell will be tricky. Mostly, folks out here aren't up for moving. They think their land has value, so they hold onto it. Usually, they think it's worth more than it is. When they realize it isn't, the myth is shattered, and they sell."

"And how do we do that?"

Harvey looks at a hawk sitting on a fencepost. "It is avarice that most reveals the soul's longing. It is never enough to use. It must possess. Every man seeks to own, even if not by placing his name on a deed or a bill of sale, but by finding a way to manifest his control. The time to sell comes when avarice abounds, and those who want control finally exert it."

Rob doesn't respond and looks straight ahead.

The average Douglas fir in western Oregon grows between a quarter and a half inch in diameter and two feet in height each year. Donald figured if he staved off the deer, kept the scrub cleared, and made sure his trees were watered even during the heat of August, they would grow at least twice as fast. He wasn't wrong. Ten years later, the trees were tall enough and Donald found himself thinning his nascent evergreens. The stand had begun to resemble a real forest, as the narrow crowns of the Doug firs towered over the oaks and maples nearby.

Every year, Donald measured the trees' diameter at breast height, which he had been told was an "official" way to estimate the overall size of the trees, volume, and board feet if logged.

Like marking the growth of children on a door frame, he would carefully measure the circumference of each tree four and a half feet off the ground, calculate the diameter, and write the number in a three-ring notebook. Despite a limited formal education, he was quick with numbers and translated the diameter into board feet before calculating the value of his trees based on lumber prices.

Around this time, the mill in Crawfordsville shut down, as did many of the mills up and down Willamette Valley. Donald took jobs where he could, laboring at construction sites, unloading trucks at the feed store, and cleaning the elementary school after hours. And while he made enough to feed and clothe Billy, there were times when his limited income wasn't enough to pay for life's incidental expenses. When the truck needed a new radiator, a snag punched a hole in the roof during a storm, or Billy broke his arm in gym class, Donald turned to his trees for help. A load of logs would fetch enough to tide the family over for a few months and cover unexpected expenses.

Whenever he cut a few trees, Donald would quickly replant, replacing one tree with several and over time, thinning their number to ensure at least one or two would mature. Occasionally, he planted hemlock or pine, and on rare occasions, cedar. Each species of tree grew at different rates, which allowed some to reach the canopy before others. In time, the homestead was completely forested, with some trees growing furtively as others burst toward open sky.

Harvey feels giddy as the Ford makes its way from the Aegolius Valley back to I-5. Rob is appropriately quiet but asks if Harvey needs to stop and take a leak. Harvey doesn't want to stop. His mind is in motion. On his phone he looks up wholesale lumber prices, housing starts, supply chains, prices at Home Depot for plywood, and International Paper production targets. His mind races. Where others see a forest, Harvey sees trees. Valuable, leverageable, sellable trees.

As they merge onto the freeway north, Harvey taps his phone. "Tell me about the spotted owl."

Rob sighs. "For over a hundred years, people here logged. The bigger the trees, the better. Supplied timber to the whole country. Most of the forests in the Pacific Northwest were cut at one point or other. Lots of jobs. Money flowed into communities, government coffers were fat, life was good. But no one understood what was being lost."

Rob pulls out a can of Copenhagen from his shirt pocket. With the flick of his wrist, he taps his knuckle on the can and pulls off the lid. He pinches tobacco from the can and stuffs it under his lip. He offers the can to Harvey, who declines. Rob puts the can back in his pocket. "The oldest trees were mostly wiped out. It's hard to find them anymore. And all the critters that lived in the old growth supposedly got wiped out too. Back in the '70s, someone finally noticed."

Rob spits a large wad of tar-colored saliva and tobacco out the window. "A kid at Oregon State in the late '60s wrote his thesis about how the northern spotted owl might be a 'signal species.' Which is to say the health of the owl populations signaled the health of the forest. Some government types picked up on that, along with the environmental movement, and had the thing declared endangered. As if the damned bird ever *wasn't* endangered. Soon, there wasn't any logging in old-growth forests, then younger forests, and eventually, any government forest. Shut down the whole industry."

Harvey nods. "That was on public lands, yes?"

"That's right. Most logging in those days took place on U.S.

Forest Service land. When the owl was declared threatened, those forests were largely off limits."

Harvey taps his phone faster. "And what happened to timber prices?"

Rob laughs. "Well, they rose. All those little houses sittin' on a few acres, the ones that were timber rich and cash poor—well, back in the '80s and early '90s, folks were so sure they'd lose their timber, they cut down anything and everything they had."

"Their own trees?"

"Yep. On their own land."

Harvey stops tapping his phone and looks out the window. "What if private landowners couldn't cut down their own trees?"

Rob shrugs. "Might make more sense to sell."

Harvey sees another hawk on a fencepost. Slowly, he looks back at the road. "Just need some creative incentive."

As DONALD'S TREES GREW, so did his family. A year after William was born, Marlene delivered a girl, Stacy. This time, Donald was present, standing awkwardly outside the birthing suite of the Linn County Hospital.

Donald was rigid as a father, while Marlene wore the mantel of nurturing mother. William was put to work at an early age, feeding the chickens, slopping the pig, and watering the small garden behind the house. Contemplative and careful, Stacy liked to read. By the time she was four, nearly all the children's books at the Linn County Library had been consumed by her never-ending appetite to pronounce a new word or follow a narrative.

In 1976, the year the nation celebrated its bicentennial, Marlene gave birth to her third child, Ezekiel. Her contractions started easily enough, but by the time Donald had piled the kids into the truck to head to the hospital in Lebanon, it was apparent something was wrong. Marlene was as white as a ghost. As he lifted her into his arms and carried her into the emergency room, a ribbon of blood ran down her leg. The nurses and doctors put her on a gurney and rushed her through a set of stainless-steel doors. Less than an hour later, Ezekiel was delivered.

Moments after his birth, Marlene died.

AND THERE THE little house sits—as much a part of the landscape as the rocks, the trees, and the brush. Rooted in thick clay and river rock, it's enmeshed in the forest like the giant trees surrounding it. Though visibly a part of the landscape, it remains apart, not merely the vestige of time and nature, but a sign of something more mercurial, ethereal. It roots itself in the soil deeper than the trees, down through the cracks in the bedrock, clinging to the very soul of the earth itself. The house with its tin roof and clapboard siding, dirty and decaying, is the remnant of a dream, an embodiment of one man's struggle to find a place in the world, a tiny corner of the great globe he could once and forever call his own.

CHAPTER TWO

"For the fate of the sons of mankind and the fate of animals is the same. As one dies, so dies the other; indeed, they all have the same breath, and there is no advantage for mankind over animals, for all is futility."

— *ECCLESIASTES 3:19*

NEAR THE HEADWATERS of the Aegolius, nestled in a grove of cedars and pines, there is a basin carved into the cascade basalt where the nascent stream pools. The water there is brown during the winter rains, when the muck is thick, and fallen leaves and needles rot and sink to the bottom of the swollen pond. In the spring, it becomes bloated with the melting snowpack and the water is so clear you can see all the way to the bottom. As summer heat descends, the water is infested with water skimmers and larvae—even the deer won't drink from it.

If you throw a stone into the pool, the water comes alive, roiling and bubbling like a giant pot of muddy stew left too long on the stove. As the waters calm, a deep, guttural note echoes off the walls of the forest. And as it fades, a second reverberates across the water, followed by a third, and then a fourth. Soon, a great chorus thunders through the cedars and pines, bouncing from rock to tree far across the Aegolius Valley. Then, as if an invisible maestro has signaled a coda, the pond grows silent and the water stills.

During the height of the din, if you stare at the pond and try to pinpoint the source of the sounds, you can't make out a thing, just water and brambles and detritus and muck. The hundreds of frogs you know are there, right there in front of you, bellowing out note after note, trumpeting like the French horn section of the forest philharmonic, are completely invisible. They cry out at the top of their lungs, heard and unseen.

As FRED RICHARDS makes his way up the Aegolius, he's hot, dirty, and tired. He's wearing his dark green, REI bucket hat and an Oregon State University Athletics sweatshirt soaked with sweat. But he doesn't notice. His eyes dart back and forth from the base of one tree to another like a hound dog following a scent. He scurries around picking up pieces of bark, needles, and cones, carefully examining each. A magnifying glass hangs from a string around his neck, and he intermittently picks it up to look at something and then drops both the glass and forest debris before moving on to the next inconspicuous item.

Richards is searching for his opus, his apogee, his raison d'etre, the climactic culmination of a career dedicated to the biological diversity of the North American temperate forest. He is undeterred by the heat, the wayward detritus in the creek bed, and the mosquitoes that have taken a liking to the back of his neck. He is paunchy, balding, and bearded, in the way all emeritus professors of biological sciences should be. Decades spent teaching in lecture halls, staring into a microscope, writing grants, writing papers, writing textbook chapters, writing and writing and writing, have left Richards nearsighted, short-winded, and more than a little cynical.

But not today. Not here. Today, Richards is in his element, in the place where biology comes alive, where he first discovered the wonders of the living world, the delicate intricacies of all things. In the dirt and the mud, between the roots and fallen branches, where the moss and lichens eat away at the rubble of the forest floor, he finds himself. Deep down in the muck, he truly sees himself and feels that if he can understand how it all works, how the stuff of life is meshed, he will discover a central meaning.

And in the heart of that meaning is his legacy, the thing to make Dr. Fredrick J. Richards a name immortalized by biology students from time immemorial. Frederick J. Richards, discoverer of that thing that so thoroughly defines the careers of the greatest emeritus professors of the biological sciences: a new species.

Behind Richards are two mostly disinterested graduate students. Theresa Houghton has been working on her PhD for three years and needs—badly needs—to find a subject for her thesis. Nigel Khurma, one year further along, has a thesis, but he desires to be in Richards' good graces when the time comes to defend it. And he is quite attracted to Theresa, with whom he taught the Biology 101 seminar a year ago.

They trail along behind Richards, pretending to be attentive to the same bits of biological refuse the professor is examining while secretly wondering why they chose the doctoral program in the biological sciences, especially since it meant hiking through fetid, mosquito-infested underbrush looking for a sasquatch or snipe or whatever-fucking-roadkill the professor thinks he is going to find.

At midday, the trio stops. Nigel and Theresa sit at the foot of an oak tree and share a bottle of water. Richards pulls out a paper map and looks closely at a series of marks on it. He crosses off some and circles others. Nigel edges closer to Theresa, who doesn't seem to mind. He pulls a small notebook out of his pack and hands it to her, suggesting she write down some thoughts about thesis topics they can discuss later, preferably with a bottle of wine in a small Italian restaurant not far from the apartment she shares with two other roommates.

Then here comes the oddest bunch. Fat feller in a green hat, dark-skinned Injun, and some frumpy girl in a yellow shirt. See 'em comin' from clear down in the dank part of the wood. Lookin' for something, they were. And funny they were. Fatso runs ahead, the two kids tiptoein' behind, looking bored. I was about to send the dogs out and have 'em run off, but then I think, maybe I let it go, if there's something they wanted.

At the base of a grove of tall firs, Richards sees it for the first time. Right there, in the middle of a small pile of needles meshed like a pin cushion. It's tiny, smaller than he expected. He stops and sits. For the first time, Nigel and Theresa are interested, and they sidle up to Richards to have a look.

Richards takes out a plastic bag and a pair of rubber gloves and picks it up by its stunted tail. It's darker gray than he expected, but everything else is exactly right. The feet, the discolored snout. It's his white whale. He looks with the magnifying glass, turns the creature over, and examines the light gray underbelly. The creature squirms and grips his rubber glove with its tiny claws. Richards pulls out a camera, a small, high-resolution device he carries in his pocket. He begins to take pictures of the little mammal sitting on his finger. He takes some videos, then puts the animal back on the ground next to the nest of needles. For several minutes, he follows it with the camera as it makes its way up a tree. It moves slowly at first, clinging to the bark in the same way it clung to Richards' glove. Then, as a shadow falls across the tree trunk, the animal freezes, barely visible against the bark of the tree, before it suddenly races skyward into the canopy.

They followed the crick bed pretty darn close. Didn't really seem to know what they's looking fer. So I watched and let 'em come up the homestead way. Figure they'd get here in time.

I seen it then. The fat feller, he picked up one of them nests the tree voles make. And he's all happy and 'cited like he never seen one before and it's the biggest, baddest thing he ever saw. I ain't never seen someone make such excitement over a little thing like that.

Richards stands quietly for a moment after looking up into the tree. He takes off his hat, revealing his balding, sweaty head, and removes his glasses as they begin to fog up. Theresa and Nigel stand behind, following his gaze up the tree. Both suddenly remember they are doctoral students in the Department of Biological Sciences on an expedition to find a new species. The trio stands quietly and doesn't speak for several minutes.

I finally decide to sick the dog on 'em. Not cause they's doin' anything scandalous. Can't see a man decidin' to let anyone walk over his property. The dogs ain't goin' to hurt 'em, only get their attention. They don't look like gun-carryin' types, but just in case they is, I grab the twenty gauge and follow.

Richards, Nigel, and Theresa freeze when they hear the dogs. Two large, black labs bark and snarl, barreling through the underbrush and descending like maelstroms rolling down the river valley. They corner the trio. Theresa grabs Nigel's arm and steps slightly behind him, something Nigel would normally find alluring. Given the circumstance, he would feel better if Theresa were the one standing in front. Richards reaches into his pack and pulls out a can of bear spray. He points it at the dogs but doesn't press the red button to unleash the noxious, blinding jet. The dogs circle and snarl, herding their human stock closer and closer together.

Don Karlsson's voice booms from the edge of the creek. "All right now, back off. Come here. Back off."

The dogs stop barking, turn, and run to him. Richards puts the bear spray back in his pack and puts his hat back on.

Theresa doesn't move and continues clinging to Nigel, who isn't certain whether he has wet himself.

As Don approaches the intruders, the dogs circle, tails wagging, tongues out, looking more like household pets than Cerberus. The closer he gets, the taller Don appears. He is wearing a white tee shirt, Dickies, red suspenders, and caulk-soled boots. His posture is as ramrod straight as his crew cut.

So, I call the dogs off 'em. "They ain't as vicious as they sound," I says. Fat one looks like he's gonna have a coronary, sweatin' an all. The girl looks like she's about ready to cry, and the boy looks like he'd peed himself. I tell 'em they was on private property. Fatty says they was a hunt for a special critter, which I thought was some kinda bigfoot sasquatch type deal. Then they showed me a vole nest and said that's the critter. I says, "Well, that one of them tree voles," and they got real excited, which was the funniest damn thing I ever heard. I told them the voles ain't new—I been seeing them since I was a kid. We called 'em owl food. Then Fatty asks if I could find him one.

Don looks up into the canopy of the forest. Richards, Theresa, and Nigel follow his gaze. His piercing eyes examine one tree and then another, and finally, another. One of the dogs, tail wagging, bumps into Nigel, who stumbles backward into Theresa, who falls to the ground. She gasps as the dog licks her face.

In one, swift movement, Don raises the shotgun toward a spot on the tree, fires the gun, and then again. The dogs don't respond to the blast, but Nigel cowers. Theresa, still sitting on the ground, covers her ears. Richards doesn't seem to notice the blasts but looks with interest as something falls out of the tree.

Dropped three of them voles right out the tree. Fat feller puts on these gloves and picks them up like they some kinda precious thing. I tell him I can pop a bunch more, but he says that's enough. Puts the ones I popped in these little plastic bags with red tags. When he's done, he gets all emotional like. Says he got some dust in his eye. All over a dad burnt vole.

Richards asks Don if he can take one of the vole nests. Don looks serious for a moment and then laughs. Nigel, who is terrified, helps Theresa up. Richards ignores Don, carefully picks up one of the vole nests, puts it in a Ziplock bag, and stuffs it into his pack. He shakes Don's hand and thanks him for helping.

That's how it all started, see. Man comes in your house actin' like he's there to check somethin' out, but really, it's somethin' of yours he wants. An' he's gonna take a little bit, or borrow it, or let me hold that thing for a quick sec. I'll give it right back. But really, he ain't givin' nothin' back, see. It's a ruse. He's there to take and only take. It's all avarice and mendacity on the inside. But you don't see it in the moment. He's gonna take it from you, take it all and leave you with nothin' but the guts of your soul. And all you can do is watch.

WHEN ZEKE WAS BORN, *he was a tiny thing. He wasn't supposed to be that small, but he comed early.*

Marle was bleedin' bad when we got to the hospital. I drove up to the front door and ran inside to get a wheelchair. I get her into the emergency and a nurse saw her and started yellin', and a whole bunch of folks come runnin'. They grabbed Marle and rushed her back to someplace in the bowels of the hospital. That was the last time I saw her.

They stuck the kids and me in a little room off the lobby. It had a couch, a couple chairs, and a picture of Jesus on the wall. Stace and Billy fell asleep on the floor. I keep comin' out and askin' where Marle is, what's happening, and gettin' all up in people's business. Finally, a doc comes out and sits me down. He tells me they got the baby out, but Marle didn't make it. Lost too much blood, he says.

I don't remember much after that. Someone asks me if I want to see her. I says yes but meaning, I want to see her alive. I followed some lady back to a room with white tile walls and a bed in the middle. They covered up everything with a sheet except Marle's face. She was gray, like a cloud of smoke, her eyes half shut so you could see how lifeless she was. Her lips were slightly open like she had breathed life out of her body. I turned away, but the image was forever burned into my mind. I try to forget and remember Marle alive and whole. But I see it still. Even now.

After a time, I went to the hospital cafeteria where Billy and Stace were eating french fries and coloring with the new crayons a nurse gave them. I sat down and didn't say anything. Stace tried to give me a french fry, but I left it.

I don't remember how long we stayed there, the kids and me. I tried to think of how to tell them Marle was gone. Then a nurse come out and ask me if we want to see Zeke.

We go into the nursery, and Zeke is so small he barely fits in the crook of my arm. Stace is immediately taken with him, wantin' to hold him, and even Billy seems interested.

Then it hits me. Marle ain't comin' home. I ain't never again goin' to see her standing on the porch, or walking through the garden, or pulling water out the crick. She's never gonna do that thing where she scrunches up her nose and makes Billy laugh. Ain't gonna brush Stace's hair or bake cookies or climb into bed and curl up in a ball. It's all past. All gone.

And there's the kids. Now there's three of 'em. Somehow, I've got to tell them, but I can't. Can't say nothin'. I'm mute, sittin' like a bump on a log. I can't find the words. Can't figure out how to start. So, I spit it out, like I'm saying there's mashed potatoes for dinner. Like it's goin' to rain, so put on your coat, or you need to wash your face before bed.

But Stace and Billy are enthralled with little Zeke and act like they barely even heard me. So, I say it again. Stace nods and says Mom just had a baby so course she ain't comin' home. And Billy's blowin' on Zeke's nose, so he scrunches up his face. I didn't know what else to say so I didn't bring it up again.

Zeke had Marle's eyes and her nose. They say babies don't smile when they are first born, but I swear Zeke smiled like Marle when he looked up at me. Maybe Marle knew she was dying and tried to leave a little bit of herself— the little raise of an eyebrow, the dimple in a cheek, the spark in his eye. It was all Marle.

After a week passed, Billy and Stace began to realize their mother wasn't coming home. Stace seemed to understand first—she was always ahead of the boys. When the gravity of it started to weigh on her, she brooded about, absorbing the fact that Marle was gone. One afternoon, it finally seemed to hit her. Suddenly, she stands up and says, "Mom's dead, right?" I ain't certain if I'd come to terms with it yet, least not until that very moment. I nodded and put my hand on her cheek. She gets teary-eyed and breathes heavy like someone's punched her in the gut. Then, she takes a breath, stands up real straight, and goes to the kitchen. Didn't mention it again for a week.

When I explained it to Billy, he'd say "okay" and then five minutes later ask when Mom was comin' home. When Stace talked to him, it seemed to sink in. She told him people are like leaves on a tree. They grow in the spring, turn colors in autumn, and fall off in the winter. I'm not sure why she thought of leaves. Maybe it's something Marle said to her, or maybe it seemed like an easy way to explain it to Billy. Whatever the reason, it got through and Billy cried and cried and cried. He cried for what seemed like a week. Stace or I would hold him, calm him down, and then a few minutes later, he'd start to cry again.

Zeke never knew anything other than his momma was dead. He didn't have a mom, and all he had was Billy, Stace, and me. He knew we'd do the best we could fer him, but it wasn't quite the same. Still, he never seemed too bothered by it. When someone asked where his momma was, he'd smile and say she died but was never really gone. She's here, he'd say, you just can't see her.

When I got Marle's ashes, I took them up to a real nice spot on top of a hill where the crick rolls off a little shelf and pours down into a basin of stone. Marle liked to go to that clearing in the late summer and have a sit. I dug a deep hole, put part of her ashes in, and let the rest out into the creek. The bed of the creek was a dark clay, and as I poured the ash into the water, it settled out in a long, white ribbon on the bottom, stretching down the creek bed as far as the eye could see.

Billy hated goin' near Marle's ashes. He never talked about her. Every year, the kids and I'd go and sit near her headstone and say a prayer. On the walk up, Billy always walked slow, kind of meandered along, like he'd done somethin' bad and was headed off to get a spankin'.

Stace would take Zeke's hand and march ahead of me. The same way Billy hated the waterfall and the clearing, Stace seemed drawn to it. When she got older and somethin' happened at school, or she felt bad, she'd go up there and have a sit. She closed off to me and Billy and Zeke, and I'd sneak up and hear her talkin' to Marle. I always felt bad then, 'cause she wasn't talkin' to me. Somehow, I hadn't been able to fill Marle's shoes when she needed me to. But I know'd Marle was listening, so I'd sneak right back and leave Stace and Marle to their talk.

I'd told Billy early on after Marle's pass that he needed to step up and make sure Stace and Zeke was okay. He's the oldest and without their mother, the other two was goin' to need someone besides me to look after 'em. Billy'd rub his hands and nod and puff out his chest like he'd already grown.

I ain't certain whether a person has a soul, or if there's a heaven, or if we all just turn back into the stuff we were made from. Maybe it's all the same thing. Whatever the case, Marle's a part of the place where her ashes were laid down. Just like the trees and the rocks and the water. She is that place. Zeke's right. Marle's dead, but she never really left. And ain't God or hell or nothin' goin' to take her away.

TIM HAMFORT DRIVES his truck up the Aegolius Highway. He's proud of the truck, a 1999 Kenworth T800 with a 1974 lift axle. Every week, he washes it and wipes the chrome off by hand. He posts pictures on Facebook the way his neighbors post pictures of their dogs or kids, complete with videos of thirty-two or forty-foot logs being dropped by a loader onto the bed between the stakes. He doesn't mind that his soft belly rubs against the leather-covered steering wheel, or that his left knee gives a bit when he steps out of the cab. He sees his image whenever he stares at the chrome plate on the side of the cab, and he smiles.

As he pulls off the highway onto Don Karlsson's drive, Tim pumps the horn. Don is standing next to a loader, tall and rigid, with dark, piercing eyes, a shock of crew-cut white hair, and red suspenders stretched across a white tee shirt. His jeans are worn and frayed, and his Redwing boots are scuffed and torn.

Tim parks and climbs out of the cab. He doesn't smile as he walks toward Don but moves a toothpick from one side of his mouth to the other and back again. "How much you got for me?"

Always can rely on Hamfort. Just like his daddy. Always on time. Drives that truck with a gleam and a smile on his face. Ain't never missed a load.

Don barely flinches. "'Bout three loads." He gestures toward a pile of logs behind the loader. "4,500 a load, I'm guessing."

Tim stuffs his hands in his pockets. "Those are some big hauls."

Don looks at his trees. "Taxes went up this year. Payin' fer a new road or school or such."

Tim's eyes narrow. "Or lining their pockets."

Don nods. His tall, rigid frame moves toward the pile of logs. As if choreographed, Tim walks back to his truck and begins backing it up. The ground is hard, and the truck has little difficulty rumbling along the dirt, worn flat by yearly incursions into the same space.

Tim locks the truck in place and jumps back out. He watches as Don works the loader and drops each log between the stakes. When the bed is full and Don turns off the loader, Tim throws a cable over and cranks the chain to tighten the bundler. He secures a red flag on the end of the longest log. "Two more?"

Don nods.

The ritual has begun. Tim will take the logs to the mill in

Springfield, where another loader will hoist them onto piles ready to be milled. Then, Tim will return for another load and then another. He'll chew up three toothpicks in the process, one for each load. After the final load, he'll leave an invoice with Jim Schonell in the little office next to the mill.

Tim understands the ritual. He's made a nice living hauling trees from various landowners to the few remaining sawmills in Willamette Valley. No one gets rich, but it's enough to own a house and raise some kids.

At the mill, the scaler measures the diameter of each log before it's unloaded. He's a short, squat fellow with a tobacco chaw pressed into his left cheek. He looks at the logs and assesses their length once they've all been piled together. He doesn't write anything down. Tim can't decide whether he respects the scaler for doing the math in his head or if he doesn't trust the process. In either case, he won't get a say. He'll be told what number will be on the invoice. It's an important number that will determine whether Tim takes his kids to the Chinese restaurant in Brownsville, where they'll break apart their fortune cookies and question why it might be better to "ask twice than lose once" and "offer courtesy as a welcome mat." It will decide whether he buys a new pair of steel-toed boots or Dickies. The number will determine if he drives his family to the coast at the start of crabbing season and plucks Dungeness from a pot on dock at the Hamilton Hotel. He always holds his breath while he opens the invoice.

Two weeks after he sees the number, a check will arrive. Tim will meet Don in the lobby of Western Bank. Don always complains about timber prices: "Why the hell are we importing so much timber from the goddamned Canadians?" He'll show Don the invoice with the number and the check. He'll multiply the number by 0.85. Don will stare silently as Tim does the math then tears off the check and hands it over. Don will spend a moment studying it as though he needs to make certain the paper is real.

Never trust a man with money. Not that he ain't trustable, but when money's involved, his perspective can get sideways. Put him in charge of helpin' build a house or plowing yer drive, and if it's out of the goodness of his heart, he'll be honest and clear. But give him a dollar, and you'll never know what he'll do. Money sullies a man. Puts a shade on his heart and blinds what he knows is right.

When the check is cashed, Tim takes his cut, and the rest is deposited into Don's account. Five months later, Don will walk into the Linn County Courthouse in Albany, write a check to the Linn County Tax Collector on the third floor, and receive a green receipt stamped "paid." Then, he's done with the whole business until next year, when the ritual will begin again.

Billy would get the other two ready before the school bus come. He'd help them get dressed, find breakfast, and make it outside on time. The bus stopped at the edge of the drive, which was a good third of a mile from the house. The drive snaked through the trees, out of sight of the house. I 'magine it was scary at times, especially in the winter when it was dark, and the three of 'em had to make their way through the dark woods and all. But they did. And it made 'em strong.

Whenever I'd see the kids walking home from school, Zeke would walk behind the other two. Sometimes kids get all worried or flustered when they're alone, but not Zeke. He'd meander along, minding himself, looking at the trees and the birds. I'd told Billy he was in charge, since he's the oldest. He did his best to keep an eye on Stace and Zeke, but sometimes Zeke would see somethin' and run off to one place or another. But I knew Stace would keep an eye on Billy as much as he'd keep an eye on her and Zeke, so with all of them watchin' out for each other, they'd make it through all right.

The school only called me 'bout Stace once to say she'd punched a boy. That was how they'd told it, but when I come and get her, I saw two boys, maybe twice her size, one with his nose bloodied and the other with a shiner. Principle Stanton tells me Stace attacked them two boys, and "girl's changes" were probably what caused it. She needed some "guidance," he says. I tell him the only way Stace could ever beat on anyone was if they'd done somethin' to her. And if I found out what they had done, them boys wouldn't only need to worry 'bout Stace. Stanton didn't say nothin' after that.

When we get home, I asked Stace what happened, but she didn't tell me nothin'. Didn't get an answer until Billy come home with Zeke. He says those boys were takin' lunch from a couple of the smaller kids at school. Stace tells one of them boys to give it back. They laugh at her, so she lets 'em have it.

Every morn' I'd russ 'em out of bed, get some food in 'em, and send them on their way. They'd stop by Mrs. Ross's place and wait for the school bus there. She'd sometimes give 'em some oats or toast on account of her kids being grown, and she missed feedin' them in the morning. So, the kids would get fed twice before they even got near school. The lunch at school was free, 'long as I remembered to sign 'em up at the start of the year.

I'd get home smellin' of gas and wood chips 'bout the same time as the kids was gettin' back from school. After I'd get home, I'd fire up the stove and try an' cook 'em something. The kids had chores to do and homework after that.

When they got older and Crawfordsville Timber Company started cuttin' back on crews, I worked swing at the mill, which meant I'd get the kids out early in the morning, but they were on their own after school. They did good, most times.

FRED RICHARDS HADN'T PLANNED on learning to pilot a drone. But after he'd talked to a graduate research assistant in the Department of Forestry, he finally succumbed to the idea of mastering the dials and joysticks on the handheld controller. The first two crashed into piles of electric motors and bits of copter blade before he finally understood he couldn't simply stop, set the controller down, and look at the instruction manual while the drone was still in the air.

But here it is.

Nigel sits on the ground next to Richards, holding the drone. As he twirls the blades and moves the camera back and forth on the base, he looks out over the forest below. He can see the Aegolius Highway, the creek, and even the railroad—or at least, what's left of it. This is why he chose biology. He hates classrooms. And laboratories. Groomed for law school, he had rebelled.

Richards motions to set the drone down. Nigel puts it on a stump and steps away. The drone suddenly comes alive as the blades start to spin. Nigel covers his ears as it lurches upward, moving in fits and starts as Richards works the controller.

The whirring blades make their way skyward and move away from the ridge like a large hummingbird. Richards and Nigel watch on a laptop, recording video from the camera on the drone. As they watch, Nigel looks over a forest service map he's spread out in the back of the small pickup, trying to ascertain what part of the forest the camera sees. The map is divided into squares. As the drone flies, Richards rattles off a series of letters and numbers, which Nigel diligently writes into each square.

"R, 6, 14, A 1" is followed a few minutes later by "L, 4, 6, B 32."

And so it goes. The emeritus professor of biological sciences doesn't particularly like the idea of the drone. Light aircraft with a professional survey crew would have been his preferred choice, but funding, the unanimity of the research oversight committee, and his own students suggested the drone was the better choice.

The drone slowly makes its way up the valley. It hovers as

Richards dictates numbers to Nigel, then zips forward, stops, and hovers again.

Nigel doesn't notice, but Richards gradually becomes more intent as the drone moves closer and closer to where the tree voles were discovered.

When the drone reaches the Karlsson homestead, Richards stops talking for a moment. He stands, though his eyes don't move from the laptop, then mutters, "What the hell?"

Nigel looks at the laptop. He's never heard Richards swear.

The drone is hovering over a section of Aegolius Creek. It takes a moment for Nigel to recognize the thicket where Richards found the first vole. As the drone rises and pans out, he sees a series of stumps.

Richards starts fiddling with the laptop. "Where's the camera on this thing?"

Nigel shakes his head. "You're using the camera right now."

"No, I mean how do I capture these images? We have to document this, record it!" Richards sounds desperate.

Nigel touches a key on the laptop and points at a shape in the corner of the screen.

"What's that?" Richards asks.

Thought it was a buzz saw when I heard it. Whirly dervish got the dogs riled up. Buzzing up and down, moving and stoppin'. Raisin' Cain.

Nigel punches another key, and the camera zooms in. The shape is too dark to make out.

I know they're lookin' at me. No idea who they are, but it don't matter. A man shouldn't have to hide if he ain't doin' nothing wrong. Shouldn't have to worry about anyone lookin' over yer shoulder. But you do.

Richards brings the drone down to get a closer look. He and Nigel stare at the screen. Richards moves the focus in and out. The shape doesn't change.

There comes a point where you had enough. They look at your land, your home, your livelihood, and say, "I think I want some of that." And when you refuse, they try and take it. Not all at once. No, sir. They're like termites, eat up a little here, little there. You don't notice at first, see. It's so small. But them termites will take your house.

The shadow gets bigger and starts to come into focus. Richards brings the drone in closer.

Nigel watches the shadow move. "Sasquatch?" he wonders aloud. Now there would be a biological find.

You have to stop 'em before they start. Keep 'em out. People who look always want. They say they're havin' a stare, but it's really about envy. Yup. That one. One of the seven deadlies. Even heaven itself looks down and covets.

As the drone descends, the shadow moves from behind a tree. It takes a moment for Richards to make out the shape of a man. Surprised, he stands and takes a partial step backward, away from the laptop.

Nigel squints at the screen. "That's the guy!"

Don comes into sharp focus, as does the shotgun, which Richards and Nigel see him raise right before the screen goes dark.

WHEN STACE STARTED SCHOOL, she and Billy would take Zeke down to Joyce Callahan's house and pick him up on the way back. If I finished work early enough, I'd get him myself, which didn't happen often, but I always felt better when I did. Joyce helped with the kids on the regular, bein' she didn't have any of her own.

Gettin' to the Callahan house either meant they'd have to walk a half mile down the highway, with cars and trucks zippin' by, or on the path that goes down by the crick and back up over the ridge. Since the highway weren't safe, I had the kids take the ridge. Most days that'd be fine, but in the late winter, mornings were dark, and they'd have to march up over the hill without seein' much. At first, I'd worried 'bout that, but them kids never complained.

Billy told me he liked goin' to school when it's dark. Said he felt safer when it's dark. I asked what he meant by that, and he said the dark was like wearing camo when we'd go hunting—he couldn't see nothin', but nothin' could see him. Which all sounded fine until they come runnin' home to say they saw a cougar watching them from the ridge. Stace got the largest stick she could find and started yellin' and hollarin' loud. Billy put Zeke in between him and Stace and did the same. After making lots of noise, they grabbed Zeke and ran as fast as they could. When I heard what happened, I got my 30-06 and went to find it. Being territorial, cougars can sense when they've crossed into another territory, and I wanted to make damn sure it knew this was mine. It was on my grounds, and I don't tolerate predators.

CHAPTER THREE

"Leave me alone, for my days are but a breath."

— JOB 7:16

The old rail line that snakes up the Aegolius Valley is overgrown with long grass and sword ferns and covered in moss. In places the ballast is washed out, and only the rails and a few sleepers remain. Where the rail line crosses Aegolius Creek, the bridge turns dark orange as its paint peels away, and moisture from the creek oxidizes the iron trestles and mounts.

Below, the creek is deep enough that in the late spring, truant schoolchildren in boxers and cutoffs can drop ten feet from the bridge into the muddy waters. By the time school ends in early summer, the creek begins to shallow, and the children of the Aegolius don't jump until they've crawled down the muddy bank through the nettles and ferns to check the creek's depth. If they can dive down to touch the bottom, they put their shirts back on, scramble up to the rail line, and march home.

Trains with beaten cars, worn by years of loaders dumping

oversized logs between their steel stakes, used to line the railway. Never deep or wide enough to float logs downstream to the mills, Aegolius Creek was simply a hindrance to the logging companies that spent a century cutting, yarding, and milling the forests spanning the hillsides of the valley. Log trucks couldn't make their way up the narrow dirt roads to the landing where crews would park a donkey and a spar pole, send men downhill to cut, set chokers, and watch the limbed and bucked logs slowly climb the hill to the landing. On rare occasions, when trucks couldn't make it up the hillsides, the donkey, belching diesel smoke, was repositioned at the bottom of the hillside and the logs were pulled down, with great trepidation, where the rail cars sat waiting to be loaded and filled.

Three days a week the train crawled up and down the valley, always at a snail's pace, slow enough that kids could jump on the unloaded cars or put coins on the track and pick them up when they had been squashed into unrecognizable shapes.

When men in suits far away from the Aegolius created rules that slowed the timber harvests, the trains inched their way up the valley on fewer and fewer days, until they finally stopped completely.

Years after the trains left the Aegolius, people still stopped in the places where they crossed the highway. They'd stop their pickups and look up and down the tracks waiting for the rusted locomotive and dented cars. But the trains never came. And they'd turn back to the road, drive over the tracks, and wonder what exactly they were waiting to see.

LINN COUNTY SHERIFF Sherrod Jensen slowly makes his way up the Aegolius Highway. He keeps the window of his Suburban open so he can feel the cool breeze. It's a leisurely drive. He never exceeds the speed limit and sometimes slows to look this way or that, to see if so-and-so has recently purchased a new truck or if that house just-a-bit-off-the-road over there has a new occupant—and did the family that lived there really move or were they forced out?

It's not merely morbid curiosity. Jensen was elected sheriff because he is good at remembering names. And not just names, but the things behind those names, the interesting parts —the things that make a name real. For example, Jeremy Rickton drives a truck and has a big garden because his wife and kids left him, and he needs things to take care of. Lily Thompson just bought a Harley she'll never ride from Dave Smith, who needed the money for his daughter's college. Steve Lawton broke his leg when he fell off his roof while trying to clean the gutters when he was drunk. And so on. That's what got Jensen the job, names and the things behind the names. But there are some names Jensen doesn't know as well as others. Those are the hard ones. But the way Jensen sees it, a name without a story is either a potential rival or a future constituent. Even people who've done bad things vote.

Donald Karlsson is one such name. Everything Jensen knows about Karlsson is at least a decade old. He asked Reeann at the Sheriff's front desk about him. She lives up the Aegolius and works at the front desk. All she knew was that Karlsson lives there alone. His wife died years ago, and his kids are grown and gone. She said he makes a trip into town every so often but doesn't go to church or talk to anyone. It's a story Jensen's heard before. Some people live alone, out in the woods, for some reason or just trying to be alone. Some people are like that.

Which isn't to say Jensen doesn't appreciate the risk of driving out to see the man. March up to a door in town and you pretty much know what to expect. Townspeople are used to strangers knocking on their doors. But out in the rural areas, things are different. There aren't any Girl Scouts or Jehovah's

Witnesses who'd drop by to sell cookies or hand out copies of *The Watchtower*.

Out here, people don't drop by. Mistakes can happen. Come on a bit strong, or a little ham-handed, and folks might respond by grabbing a shotgun or a hunting rifle. The hardest people to relate to are people who don't want to talk.

But Jensen knows how to approach even the most militant redneck. It's an art. Be friendly, but not overly so. "Howdy, good to see you," or "Sorry to have to bother you with this old thing." Let them lead and follow along. If they start railing against the "goddammed government," let them know you're tryin' hard to keep the rest of them "lazy no-good bureaucrats and politicians" out of their hair and it's a right hard job given the lot of them up in Salem and Portland. Or if they start with the "tree-hugging, dirt-worshipin' enviros," you point out how there are a million or so board feet in those trees there and gosh darn, those Doug firs are ripe for harvesting. Soon enough, you're one of them, even with a badge on your chest.

Jensen turns the Suburban slowly up the Karlsson drive. He notices the giant trees, even by western Oregon standards —hovering over the little house. He drives up carefully. No sudden moves, nothing to provoke fear or concern. Just a friendly talk.

That's when I hear the sheriff comin' up the drive. He just meanders up, all relaxed like. Seems out for a Sunday stroll. Burly fellow. Gets out of his rig and the dogs are circling' round, tails waggin' like he's the butcher bringin' them a big ol' bone.

Jensen pats one of the dogs on the head and slowly walks toward Don. He gives his best "How the heck are ya" smile. "Great place you got here," he says. "Real nice. Sherrod Jensen. Nice to meet you." He sticks out his hand.

Ain't anything good gonna come when the lawman comes knockin'. The moment I see him, I know something's wrong. It's like before a storm, when the air smells, and the woods get quiet. One of the kids in trouble?

Doubtful. Poachers? Wrong time of year. Jewett's horse got loose again? Not really a sheriff kind of problem.

Karlsson, stone-faced, shakes Jensen's hand.

"Don Karlsson?"

"That's right."

"Real good to meet you." Jensen looks into the forest near the house. "Those are some good-lookin' trees. Don't see firs like that much anymore."

"I like 'em"

Sheriff come off real nice at first. Big burly feller with a beard. Knew right away he had some kinda bad news. Knew it was big, since he drove all the way here.

"How long you lived up here?"

"Fifty years."

"Listen, I apologize for barging in on you like this, but every so often I'm required to deliver a summons from a court."

Karlsson's brow furrows, ever so slightly.

Jensen pulls a white envelope from his back pocket and hands it to Karlsson. "It says you can't cut down any of the timber on your land."

"Wasn't planning on it."

Jensen looks relieved. "Well, I thought it was unnecessary. Why would a man want to cut down his own trees?"

Don doesn't open the envelope. He stares at it like he's never seen one before. Finally, he lifts his gaze back to Jensen. "How long?"

"How long what?"

"How long until I can harvest my trees?"

Jensen looks surprised by the question. "Well, this here is a summons to come to a hearing and talk about a Temporary Restraining Order. Means you can't cut any trees until after they've had a hearing."

Sheriff drops the bomb. Tries real hard to make it seem okay, like it's some kinda formality where I got to get permission or sign a form or some such thing. Makes me wonder why he come all the way out here to tell me about some formality. Got to get burn permits, or a license to fish and hunt. Didn't have to drive all the way up here to tell me about those.

Don looks Jensen squarely in the eye. "So, for me to cut down my own damned trees, I have to get permission from a court."

"'Fraid so."

Don stuffs the envelope in his back pocket. "Why?"

"What do you mean why?"

"Why are they doin' this?"

Jensen takes his hat off and strokes the brim. "The order says there's a critter living in these parts that needs to be protected. The court doesn't want any of their habitat removed until they've had a chance to sit down with the Fish and Wildlife Service and decide whether it's endangered or not."

That's when it dawns on me. The vole hunters. Fat son of a bitch and his no-good sidekicks. Should have put some buckshot in their backsides.

"What if I go out and harvest my own trees? What's the court gonna do after them trees are cut?"

"They'd probably throw you in jail for disobeying a court order." Jensen sighs. "Look, Don, I know it don't seem fair, but that's how it is sometimes. The thing about these orders is they'll need to have a hearing to keep the order in place. And the court requires the hearing to happen right away, so you don't have to keep waitin' if this critter isn't endangered."

That's how it is. Purty much sums things up right there. For a moment I think about findin' them vole hunters and letting 'em have it. Dirty sons of bitches. They knew what they were doing when I got a couple voles for 'em. They knew there's plenty of them damn voles in the trees. Hell, if they was really endangered, we'd need to start shootin' the owls, since they're the ones killin' most of 'em. But you can't shoot the owls, 'cause some of them were endangered. There isn't much to do to stop the damn voles from goin' extinct. Which proves they're lookin' to take something else.

Ain't about the voles, it's about the land. Which is how it's always been. Someone owns it, and someone else tries to take it. Sometimes they come with a gun and a uniform and sometimes they come with papers and a lawman. But they're always comin'.

Jensen turns toward his car. "If you want, I can give you the name of a couple lawyers in town who might be willing to fight the order. They're not too spendy, at least by lawyer standards."

Don shakes his head. "No need. I got me a bigshot lawyer already. You tell the court to git ready. I'm coming. They ain't gonna know what hit 'em."

DOUG FIRS in the Aegolius Valley experience a circuitous pattern of growth as they grow from tiny seedlings, rising only a foot or so above the forest floor, to the towering behemoths that grace the horizon.

Seedlings, barely more than a twig with a few needles sticking out of the ground, they rise just far enough before their buds become deer feed. Those that survive have few branches but grow spindle-sized trunks that shoot straight upward, barreling toward the sky to avoid further pruning from hungry herbivores. "Christmas trees they ain't" is the refrain from loggers when they see the hourglass-shaped, ten- or twelve-foot firs, tall enough to avoid the deer at their tops and bottoms. They grow slowly at first, usually dwarfed by the pines and maples, only to quickly rise in the canopy if they survive their initial childhood. As the tops begin to rise, like promiscuous teens they produce cones and pollen in quantities so great that anything left overnight in the forest on a late spring day will be covered with fine yellow powder from a dozen trees. As they reach adulthood, branches not exposed to light begin to die.

At full maturity, the tree retains only those parts capable of efficiently contributing to greater growth, so by their sixtieth or seventieth year, most Doug firs will have a crown of green and a mix of dead and live appendages below. The healthiest of them, those that survive the beetles and foreign ivy, will grow a massive trunk, so big the blade of even the longest chainsaw can barely penetrate the core of the giant. And when they finally fall, those that stood the tallest will leave a stump so large in diameter it can't be climbed or scrambled over, and the only way to find the other side is to walk around it and marvel at just how lovely it must have been when it was still standing.

"THAT'S THE GENIUS?" Vida whispers, after she's peeked through the spaces between the frosted panes into the glass-lined boardroom. At one end of the long, mahogany table, inlaid with brass and sandalwood, sits a disheveled twenty-something in a gray hoodie scrolling through his phone. He looks intentionally out of place.

"Must be," Stacy replies, shaking her head, wondering what sort of self-indulgent narcissist wandered into the boardroom looking like he just rolled out of bed. It is an anathema, a sin, to treat the boardroom with such disregard. A boardroom where she'd fought with the ferocity of a drunken logger to do something other than deliver coffee.

Immediately adjacent to the young man in the hoodie are three men in tailored gray suits. They sit perfectly ordered, like pickets on a fence.

Fifteen years of representing the firm's leftovers cases—the brother-in-law with a DUI, the wife embezzling from the family firm, the tax-dodging cousin, the cases no one else would touch—had left Stacy cold. Cold like steel. The associates she started her career with were all Ivys, top-tier grads. But they were weak, unwilling to work in the trenches. While they wrote appeals and filed briefs, she stood before state courts, bankruptcy judges, IRS agents, federal prosecutors, and every other entity where a woe-begotten client required an advocate. While her peers vacationed at the Cape, she toiled pro bono in the public defender's office, racking up time in court, learning to think on her feet, mastering the vicissitudes of judges, clients, and the law itself. State law school grads didn't get to wear sneakers and put them on the boardroom table.

Stacy straightens her blouse. She nods at Vida. "I'm gonna gut him."

Vida smirks. "You need anything?"

"Wait five minutes and bring in some coffee or water or something. If I say 'thank you,' pour a cup for me and anyone else who wants one. If I say 'yes, thank you,' pour me a cup, but no one else. Even if someone indicates they want one, don't pour it. Make him pour it himself. Whatever you do, don't pour any for the suits. Even if they ask for it. Not a drop. Got it?"

Vida nods, checks her watch, and wanders back toward the reception desk.

Stacy clears her throat and enters the boardroom. The twenty-something doesn't look up from his phone. One of the suits glances at her but doesn't stand, or even pretend to care that she's there.

One of them asks, "Could we get some water?"

Stacy ignores the question, reveling in the condescension. She feels the same satisfaction she had when Don taught her to hunt. She'd lay prone for hours next to Billy and Zeke, waiting for a bull elk to saunter into the crosshairs of her 30-06, called in by Billy's careful cadence. The best moments were those that came before pulling the trigger, when the big animal wandered closer and closer, oblivious to the danger. An apogee of stillness that could last half an hour was broken only by the reverberation of sound emanating from the rifle barrel. Stacy thought of the soil and grass camouflage she'd wear hunting whenever she put on her off-the-rack, ill-fitted blazer that never quite complemented her knit skirt and button-up blouse. Fitting for an admin or receptionist, but her attire didn't suit a rising star in one of Boston's biggest firms.

Immediately adjacent to the boardroom table are full-length windows looking out across the Boston skyline. The late afternoon sun shimmers off the harbor. Stacy walks to the windows and stares at the sailboats slicing through the waves.

"Don't worry, this won't take long," she says. She feels the suits lift their heads, realizing for the first time she isn't someone sent to serve them, but someone with the authority to negotiate.

She hears one of the suits clear his throat. "We thought we'd be discussing this case with Mr. Randall."

As she continues to stare out the windows, she hears Don's voice in her ear. *Don't flinch. Let the bull move into range.*

"Well, you're stuck with me, I'm afraid."

One of the suits sinks back into his chair. "Okay, then." She feels the tension in the room dissipate. Why would the partners send in a junior associate unless their goal was to come up with a face-saving compromise? A few dollars to cover their fees and token for the client.

Slide the safety off without moving the barrel.

Stacy turns to face the room and smiles. The three suits smile back. The gray hoodie continues to stare at his phone as though he doesn't have any role in the conversation.

The suit in the middle clears his throat. "Mr. Roy, in the interest of making this whole problem go away, would like to offer your client $25,000. He doesn't agree with your client's position and doesn't admit to any responsibility. He is simply offering this sum as an act of good faith in hopes that the misunderstanding can be resolved."

It's an opening bid, one that would have been laughable

had any of the senior partners been standing in Stacy's shoes. She slowly walks from the windows to the boardroom table and leans on one of the leather chairs surrounding it. "Now gentlemen, I think we can do better than that. Mr. Roy runs a billion-dollar company built on technology stolen from my client. I think he can afford a bit more."

Let the bull move just a bit closer.

The middle suit looks at the suit on his left, who nods. The middle suit clears his throat again, as though he's signaling his displeasure at Stacy raising the ante.

Squarely in the crosshairs. Breath slowly. Relax the shoulder.

Stacy turns her head and looks at the hoodie. "We have Mr. Roy's emails admitting to stealing the laptop. We have a video of him bragging to his little friends about it. We have copies of the original code and evidence he didn't write it."

Mr. Roy, hoodie and all, suddenly looks up from his phone with a wry smirk on his face. "And there isn't a thing anyone can do about it."

The suit closest to him raises his hand. "What Mr. Roy means is that the patent is in his name, and the laptop currently can't be found."

The middle suit chimes in, "Property Law 101. There isn't a case to be made that your client owns anything."

Don't pull the trigger. Gently squeeze.

Stacy smiles. As if on cue, Vida enters with a carafe and paper cups. "Coffee?"

Stacy pulls out the chair next to Mr. Roy and sits. "Yes, thank you." Vida pours Stacy a cup of coffee, ignores the rest of the room, sets the carafe down in the middle of the table, and walks out. The suits are suddenly aware they aren't negotiating with a junior associate.

The moment the gun fires, the bull won't run. Instead, he'll freeze, just long enough to make sure the shot doesn't miss.

Stacy swirls the coffee around in the cup. "Property law.

Your view of property law is…limited. Mr. Roy will provide substantial equity to my client, along with compensation commiserate with last year's margin."

Mr. Roy laughs. "Why would I do that?"

"Because if you don't, you'll be in jail." Stacy takes a sip of coffee, leans back, and crosses her legs.

The moment after the gun fires the elk stands for a moment, still unaware it's been shot.

"It's called Grand Larceny. Chapter 266, Section 30 of Massachusetts General Law. You violated it, and I can prove it. The sentence for property exceeding $1,200 is up to five years. Given the value of what was on that laptop, I'm guessing you'll end up doing most of that time." She takes another sip of coffee.

One of the suits smirks. "There is no way the district attorney is going to file charges against Mr. Roy. This is a civil matter. I don't care what kind of evidence you've got."

Stacy pulls a phone from her pocket and sets it face up on the conference room table. She punches in a number and turns on the speaker. A gentle voice comes on.

"Suffolk County District Attorney's Office, how can I help you?"

Stacy looks at the suit, who stops smirking. "Assistant D.A. Larry Jackson please."

"One moment."

Stacy continues to stare directly at the suits.

"This is Larry Jackson. How can I help you?"

"Larry, it's Stacy. Did you get the information I faxed over this morning?"

"Yes, I did. Good stuff. Can't wait to arrest the perp. Your guy interested in pressing charges?"

"Larry, give me one second." Stacy puts the phone on mute. She turns to Mr. Roy. "Am I interested in pressing charges?"

Mr. Roy looks at the suits, then back at Stacy. He stands up. "Fuck!" he yells. "Fuck me!" He pushes his chair back and storms out of the boardroom.

The bull falls suddenly. Dead before it hits the ground.

Stacy's eyebrows rise. "Do I take that as a no?"

The suit in the middle nods.

She unmutes the phone. "Larry, we're going to hold off for the moment. Can you give me twenty-four hours?"

"You bet. Let me know what you decide."

Stacy hangs up the phone and puts it back in her pocket. The suits look shell-shocked.

Immediately tend to the carcass. Don't waste time staring, lookin' at the damn thing. Meat starts going bad the minute the animal dies.

She stands up and walks toward the door. "I'll have papers sent over. You have twenty-four hours to send them back, signed, or I'll have to let Larry know he needs to press charges." She pauses. "And if there's any doubt, let Mr. Roy know that my client initially didn't want to make a deal. He would have given it all up to see Mr. Roy's perp walk on the evening news."

As Stacy leaves the boardroom, she walks past the reception desk. She winks and whispers "thank you" to Vida, who smirks. As Stacy turns to walk away, Vida stops her. "Oh, I almost forgot." She hands over a pink message. "There was a call for you. From your dad."

BILLY PULLS a tire off the rack. He rolls it across the cement floor to the fourth bay where a small pickup is suspended on the lift. He throws the tire on the spreader and runs the handle around in a circle, fixing it to the rim. His hands move quickly, with the certainty of experience. He pulls the finished wheel off, rolls it up next to the truck, and slides it onto the lug bolts. Before the tire is settled, his hand reaches for the drill, already loaded with the first nut, which ratchets on with a loud rip. The remaining nuts are similarly twisted into place by the drill. He sets it down and waves at Nick, who is standing by the controls for the lift.

"Drop her. She's ready for snow."

Nick hits a button, and the truck descends as the hydraulics give way to the forces of gravity.

Billy waves and yells, "Tell the fella with the Raiders jersey she's ready to go. I'm on break."

Nick nods and turns back toward the small waiting room in the shop as Billy steps through the open bay door into the cold sun. He strolls to the end of the long cinderblock building, past bays seven and eight, next to the red and white neon sign that says, "Monk's Tires." He pulls a pack of Marlboros out of his left shirt pocket and a lighter from inside his jacket.

As Billy flicks the lighter, a red Chevy pickup drives by and honks. He looks up in time to see Tom Cooney waving a newspaper. The truck slows and pulls into Monk's. Tom rolls down his window and waves the paper again.

"You see this?"

Billy shakes his head.

"Says they found some kind a new critter up at your old man's place up the valley."

Billy takes the newspaper from Tom and scans the front page. He takes a drag and laughs as he exhales. "You gotta be kidding me. Voles?"

"That's what it says. They found a new species up the Aeg. Right there on Karlsson land. Tree voles of some kind. You ever seen one of them?"

Billy hands the paper back to Tom. "Grew up shootin' 'em out of the trees. Had a BB gun when I was ten. Me and Stace used to take turns tryin' to knock 'em out of the trees."

Tom laughs. "Well, you didn't shoot enough of 'em. There's a few left."

Billy takes a drag from his cigarette. "Oh hell, there's plenty of those voles. Owls lived on 'em. We used to call them owl food."

Tom points back to the paper. "Says here they're gonna suspend all timber harvest up there until Fish and Wildlife has an accurate accounting. Your dad okay with that? He won't be able to cut any of his timber."

"Hell, my old man only cuts about a dozen trees a year on his land. Uses them to pay property taxes. Been cuttin' 'em since I was a kid. He'll cut anyone else's trees by the acre. But only a select few of his own."

"That's good, 'cause for now, he can't cut any. They're restricting all logging where they think there *might* be voles, let alone where they know they already exist."

Billy takes another drag. "Big surprise. Anything to keep a man from takin' care of his own. Goddamned tree huggers." He drops the cigarette butt onto the pavement and presses it with his boot. "I'm sure they love the voles. Just don't give a damn about people."

Tom nods. "Well, listen. If Don has any trouble, any at all, let me know. We'll get a convoy started and head up there right now. Help him cut those trees ourselves."

"They won't let me take down the trees," Don says the moment Stacy steps onto the porch. "My own goddamned trees."

Stacy smiles the same disappointed smile she'd worn when she decided the house was too small and the occupants too gruff for her to remain any longer. "It's nice to see you, too, Dad."

Don takes a half step back and stammers, "Well, ain't it great to see my daughter. All grown up and such."

Stacy folds her arms and looks at the house with a mixture

of nostalgia and disdain. She can smell the wet moss and feel the dew falling from Douglas fir needles as it wafts through air. "Hasn't changed much, has it?"

"Nope, it ain't. Hell, where's Billy? Goddammed boy knew you was coming—don't know where he went."

"I'm right here, Don." A loud voice booms from behind the trailer. With his arms filled with chopped wood, Billy looks the same to Stacy. The same ruddy face and broad shoulders, same dark hair and stubble she remembers from the last time she was home, several years ago.

"There's my sis." He drops the wood, bounds up on the porch steps, and engulfs Stacy in a giant hug. "Here from the big city to save the old homestead."

Stacy returns the hug and smiles. "Well, we'll see. Maybe if Dad weren't so ornery, I wouldn't have to come save you."

It takes a moment for Stacy to remember the subtle nuances of the little house. The broken gutter that spills water whenever it rains too hard. The cinder blocks so encased in moss they'd lost their shape. The shadows under the corrugated fiberglass overhang. The wooden brown front door with peeling paint and a handle that is clearly intended for the interior of a house. The never-ending mud and grass and moss that rises from the forest floor like tendrils from a giant dandelion saturated by spring rain.

"Where's Zeke?"

Don grimaces. "Who knows? Dadburn kid run off with his hippy-dippy friends. Probably doin' drugs or smokin' something."

Billy leans closer to Stacy. "He doesn't think we should be able to log Dad's trees. Kind of left us in a lurch. You know Zeke."

Stacy sighs. "I guess I shouldn't have assumed anything would change."

Neither man speaks.

"Show me the documents."

Don holds the door open while Billy and Stacy enter the house. On the wooden dining room table, a neatly stacked pile of papers sits next to a neatly stacked pile of envelopes.

Stacy picks up the envelopes. "Dad, you don't need to keep these."

"I need to know where they came from?"

"They came from the government. The return addresses are somewhere in Washington, DC."

Stacy sits at the tiny table and begins to read, carefully examining each piece of paper and folding it neatly when she's done. Billy and Don sit quietly across from her, waiting to hear her interpretation of the government speak. Stacy holds one of the papers up and points to a line on the front of it.

"This is a summons to a hearing which will address the Temporary Restraining Order. The government was apparently worried you'd cut down your trees and kill off all the voles, so they filed an emergency order."

Billy grimaces. "Don't they have to tell us before they file?"

"No. They don't have to tell you anything. However, because it's an emergency order that imposes a restriction on someone without due process, it's temporary and a hearing must be held as soon as possible." Stacy pauses. "Thus, the summons. You are summoned to the hearing to determine if the temporary restraining order should be turned into a preliminary injunction."

Don squints. "Preliminary to what?"

"Until there's a trial. Which could be years later. The trial will determine if the preliminary injunction should become permanent."

Don takes the paper from Stacy and looks at it carefully. After a moment, he asks, "So when does this hearing take place?"

"Later this week."

Billy clears his throat. "That soon?"

Stacy picks up another paper. "As I said, the hearing has to take place quickly because the government has restricted your rights."

Don nods. "It ain't right that a man can't do anything with his property when he wants."

Stacy crosses her legs and stares across the table at Don. "Why don't you just sell the place?"

Her father's eyes narrow. "What the hell are you talkin' about? Why in God's name would I ever sell?"

"You're getting old, Dad. There's going to be a time when you can't take care of it, let alone yourself. You could sell it, while it's still worth something, and get a place in town, near Billy or Zeke."

Don stares intently. "Marle's ashes are here. Your mother, for God's sake. Someday mine will be, too. Ain't no way anyone is going to move me off my property."

Stacy leans back and sighs. "Dad, the land will still be here, even if you're not. And we'll make sure your ashes are buried next to the creek right next to Mom's."

He scowls. "Damn kids. If you wanted you could buy it and move me out. I mean look at ya. Big city lawyer. I'm sure it'd be a half day's work for you to take the place."

"We don't want to buy it, Dad. We want to leave it and only come back to see Mom. And you. There isn't anything for any of us here."

Don crosses his arms. "I have given the land before you; come and possess the land."

Stacy leans back in her chair. "And right after that, God told Abraham to kill his son." She shakes her head. "Don't throw that biblical stuff at me."

Don stands and looks out the kitchen window. "Marle would never leave."

"Maybe not, but she would've found a way to make sure

you weren't all alone out here in the middle of nowhere. She wouldn't stand her ground, trying to fight back against time. She'd find a way to make it work. That's what mothers do. They fix things."

Don's shoulders slump. "Yeah, I know. And I'm sorry she ain't here. But she ain't." He looks down at his hands. "Only one here is me. And I ain't leavin'. I'm tied to this place, see. Tied like an old mule to a post. It ain't even so much I don't wanna leave as I can't. It'd be like rippin' the bark off a tree. Might still be standin' but nothin' alive about it." He turns back to her. "I can't fight this thing without you. Men in shirts and ties will come and take it all away. Leave me dead standin'."

Stacy drums her fingers on the table. She doesn't look at Don or Billy. "I think this might be the first time you ever asked me for help."

Don doesn't move. "Parents ain't supposed to ask for help from their own. It ain't right. But I'm askin'."

"It's okay to ask."

Don sticks his hands in his pockets. "Fair. All right. I'm askin'. Need my bigshot lawyer to fight off them shirts and ties."

Stacy looks him in the eye. "I'll help you, Dad. But I can't guarantee we won't fail. And if we do, you're going to have to move."

"We ain't goin' to fail."

CHAPTER FOUR

"Less justice, more laws."

— *CICERO*

THE FRONT IS A DIRTY WHITE—as dirty as white gets when peeling paint fails to hide the creviced T-111 siding slowly rotting away. Rich Green never felt the need to add more paint, let alone replace the decaying boards on the two-story building that sits on the corner of Mallard Road and the Aegolius Highway. The large, red plastic letters held on by a series of rusty brackets and failing wood screws are faded, but visible enough they can still be seen from a few hundred yards down the highway, declaring to the wayward truck driver or deer hunter they are near the Aegolius Market. A neon "Open" sign is lit every morning at seven o'clock and remains on until seven at night, whether he is on the premises or not, which is more frequently the case these days. The loggers who stopped by in the late afternoon to buy a six pack or case of Henry's are gone. Children from Aegolius Elementary sometimes buy candy or soda, and the hunters are there every morning in the fall and early winter.

Most days, Rich sits at the register and watches the news. A large man with a small, round face, he doesn't acknowledge customers when the chimes on the door ring. He still keeps the refrigerator stocked with Henry's, even though it's made somewhere back east and tastes like the rest of the out-of-state swill. There are earthworms and red-dyed marshmallows below the beer, on the assumption that those who stop in are more likely than not planning on becoming intoxicated while trying to catch a fourteen-inch rainbow somewhere on the McKenzie or Santiam.

A chainsaw statue of a bear stands next to a gas pump that doesn't pump gas anymore. Near the base of the bear, the artist who saw fit to use a log for something other than two-by-fours carved "Freda's Bear." Rich doesn't know what to do without the bear any more than he knows what to do without Freda. The bear guards the empty pump, and Rich guards the empty store, neither capable of moving, as the rot that comes from years sitting in cold, damp Aegolius muck slowly engulfs them both.

The Mark O. Hatfield Federal Courthouse is an edifice of granite and steel rooted in the heart of downtown Portland. A marble, gray monument to the stolid certainty of the law, it stands as an anchor of permanence, resolute and certain, unmoved by the vicissitudes of conflict that lie within. While plaintiffs and defendants, attorneys and judges, mold and shape the rules that guide the fortunes of those who enter, the building itself remains an eminence of assurance and truth.

Kent Woodson feels at ease entering courtroom number six, where the quiet is interrupted by the click of heels on the marble floor and the monotone discussions between judges and attorneys. The smell of varnish and old leather permeates the clothes of anyone who spends more than a few hours sitting in the silver and dark green chairs with rubber-soled feet neatly lined in the gallery. Kent takes his usual place behind the bar, where he can hear the shuffle of paper and taste the stale air emanating from the bench. Light gleams off the large brass seal at the foot of the bench, just enough to blind the vision of anyone sitting three feet to the right of the plaintiff's desk. More than once an attorney has been forced to halt their oration when they unknowingly stepped into the glare emanating from the great seal.

Kent's greying hair is carefully coiffed, as is his beard. He wears readers even when he's not reading, and they slide partway down his nose, projecting an air of journalistic authenticity. More recently he's simply too lazy to put them away every time he stands. Years ago, he gave up sweater vests and tweed jackets, once the uniform of the city desk journalist, for more pragmatic and comfortable button-down shirts and khakis. But even in his current attire, he appears every bit the seasoned reporter, still energetic enough to pursue a story, but circumspect with age.

Kent nods at Jerry Roberts sitting at the plaintiff's desk. Jerry looks relaxed, leaning back in his chair, legs crossed, eyes wandering around the courtroom confidently, as though he has already finished arguing the case, has received an affirmative ruling, and is ready to head down the street for a drink at Higgins. The way Kent sees things, that might just happen. As an assistant federal attorney, Jerry has an impeccable record.

Kent wouldn't be sitting in the front row of a federal courtroom listening to an esoteric case about land rights if it weren't for Jerry, who has a knack for picking cases that fit well within a larger narrative. A decade of writing stories about every carjacker, drug dealer, and miscreant who entered criminal court left Kent with the desire to write about something bigger, more meaningful. Something that could be infused with enough humanity to make a reader care about *the bigger picture*. After all, *the bigger picture* is what readers crave. *The bigger picture* is what editors like to publish, and *the bigger picture* is what wins Pulitzers. Kent can see himself holding a Pulitzer but isn't sure what he'd be holding it for; he hasn't yet been able to write about *the bigger picture*.

When the defendants arrive, Kent begins to understand why Jerry thought this might make for a great story. The plaintiff looks right out of central casting. He's tall and clean-shaven with a gray crew cut and deep-set dark eyes. His tweed gray sport coat looks a generation old and hides a blue flannel shirt, buttoned to the top. He is at once handsome and stern. His leather work boots suggest he's never been in a courtroom, or for that matter, a building more than a few stories tall. He looks as out of place as a fly on a wedding cake.

What Kent notices the most are the eyes. Deep, penetrating, obsidian black eyes. They are the eyes of something wild, something not yet civilized, something that does not understand conformity imposed by the law.

When Judge O'Connell enters the courtroom, she carries a porcelain cup of tea in one hand and her case files in the other. She doesn't look up at the claimants as she ascends the bench. After sitting, she turns and nods to the clerk, who stands and in a quick, choppy voice reads the docket. "Case number 4:2017cv0043. US vs. Karlsson."

O'Connell speaks without looking up. "Thank you. Mr. Roberts. You assert that it is necessary for the court to grant a preliminary injunction, restricting Mr. Karlsson's ability to harvest the timber on his land, based on enforcement of the Endangered Species Act of 1973. Is that correct?"

Jerry stands. "Yes, your honor."

Judge O'Connell continues. "And you can prove that your case is likely to succeed, and if a preliminary injunction is not granted, irreproachable harm will be done to the species. Is that correct?"

"Yes, your honor."

For the first time, Kent notices the plaintiff's attorney, who stands. She is intentionally unremarkable. Her gray pantsuit almost seems an illusion to feign simplicity and guilelessness.

"Stacy Karlsson for the defendant, may it please the court."

"Ms. Karlsson, I don't think I've seen you in my court before."

"Thank you, your honor. My practice is primarily in Boston." Stacy pauses. "The last time I was in your court, I clerked for Judge Brentwood. I've maintained my Oregon license ever since."

Judge O'Connell looks up quickly before responding. "Well, great to have you back."

Kent has seen enough trials to recognize a shark. Great attorneys don't wear fancy suits and recite Shakespeare. They're plain and unassuming. They blend into the courtroom as though part of the furniture, like a plants sitting in the corner, or a stack of files on a desk. In the way an alligator lurks below the surface, waiting for the right moment to let their presence be known, they stymie the opposition and expertly turn a judge or jury with a carefully placed bit of evidence or sharply worded argument. And to any well-informed court watcher, Stacy Karlsson, the plaintiff's attorney, is a shark.

Stacy clears her throat. "My client is seeking the right to cut down the trees on his property. The United States Department of Fish and Wildlife, under the Endangered Species Act, has effectively prohibited my client from selling the timber on his land. Timber he owns. Trees he planted himself with the expectation that one day they could be harvested. We ask the court to provide relief from the Department's restraining order."

Kent watches as Jerry sits up straight and whispers to the attorney sitting next to him, whom Kent assumes is from Fish and Wildlife in Washington. Kent can read his lips but doesn't need to. He knows what Jerry's saying. "Who the fuck is she, goddamnit? How the fuck did this hillbilly who lives in a trailer hire her? Why didn't someone tell me the opposing counsel was a goddamned shark? Fuck!" Jerry's face tells the tale. This case was supposed to be about Jerry—Assistant United States Attorney Jerold Roberts, environmental warrior, standing tall for animals and trees and other earth stuff. But the plaintiff isn't a timber company, it's some guy who lives out in the woods. Some guy with trees he wants to cut down. It's Jerry versus the little guy. A little guy with a shark. A fucking shark.

Judge O'Connell turns to Jerry. "Mr. Roberts, would you like to comment?"

Jerry stands, appearing a bit rattled. "Yes, your honor. A new species of mammal has been discovered in the Aegolius Creek Watershed. The United States Department of Fish and Wildlife has deemed it endangered. Since the discovery, the species has only been found on the trees growing on Mr. Karlsson's property. Until scientists can find populations in other areas, the DFW deems it necessary to prevent the logging of those trees."

Judge O'Connell responds as Jerry sits. "And why can't the state provide remuneration to Mr. Karlsson for not cutting down his trees?"

Jerry stammers, unsure of his reasoning. "Well, the thing is, your honor, if Mr. Karlsson is paid not to cut his timber, the United States would have to pay other private landowners for not doing all kinds of things. It's neither administratively nor fiscally possible."

Stacy, still standing, responds. "The new species isn't new. And it's a vole. If the United States government wishes to protect it, fine. Then pay for said protection—especially when the result is a loss to someone else."

Judge O'Connell looks at the defendant's table. "Thank you. We will proceed. Do you have any witnesses?"

Kent pulls out his empty notebook as Stacy replies, "We call Donald Karlsson."

THE GREEN TORTOISE in Eugene has seen better days. Or maybe it hasn't. The paint on its run-down, brick facade that once depicted a terrapin in running shoes might always have been in a state of evanescence, gradually fading to the color of brick.

The interior of the establishment is dark and dank, owing less to bad lighting than to the morass of sports memorabilia, beer decorations, and concert posters. Framed jerseys from local teams, outlines of last year's Final Four brackets, a neon Budweiser sign, and a framed poster from a long-forgotten Grateful Dead concert cover the walls. The benches, table, and bar appear to be hewn from expensive varnished hardwood, but closer inspection reveals the darkened wood is simply the discoloration of spilled drinks and rings caused by a patronage who doesn't use coasters.

Beyond the periphery of the main bar are several small vestibules, spaces connected to the main sitting room, many with couches, end tables, and reading lamps, well equipped for whatever small group might want to convene for an after-hours gathering. These small rooms are the reason patrons frequent the GT, overlooking its faded sign and cluttered decor. The spaces are large enough for several people, but small enough to ensure privacy and the ability to talk in hushed voices outside the din of the bar.

Inside one of Green Tortoise's anterooms, men and women huddle around a small table. Zeke sits amid the group, dressed like the others, wearing a combination of denim, flannel, and Gortex. His hair is brown and shoulder length, pulled back in a manner befitting his youth. His black eyes sparkle behind a smooth brow. As the others speak, he says little. As they emote, he remains dispassionate. As their tones become fervent, his are quiescent. He is the embodiment of a Buddha, one who has forgone enlightenment and sought incarnation in the body of a lithe forty-something, exuding tranquil stolidity from his parted brown hair to his wool socks and Keens.

"Every generation has its calling. This is ours!" a young woman proclaims. "It's our turn to take the mantle and protect the mother."

A middle-aged man in a gray jacket stands and puts his finger on the table. "Timber sales are up. If the courts won't hold the line, we'll step in."

An excitable-looking fellow with a thinning gray ponytail, who appears to be both the oldest and most animated, begins to describe standing in front of a bulldozer at Fall Creek back in the day, when the old growth was plentiful, and the stakes seemed higher. He isn't deterred by someone asking what a bulldozer was doing at a logging site.

A young woman in a jean jacket sips her IPA and pokes Zeke's knee. "I heard your father is suing for the right to cut his trees."

Zeke's face doesn't change as he responds. "Sort of. He's fighting the restraining order."

The room quiets.

A dark-haired twenty-something sporting a backward Oregon Ducks baseball cap ends the uncomfortable silence. "Your father owns a logging company?"

"No, my family has a homestead up the Aegolius Valley. He cuts a few trees every year to pay the property tax. The government filed a restraining order that has something to do with the environment and endangered species.

After the people sitting near Zeke stare at their drinks and shift uncomfortably for an awkward minute, a woman in a denim jacket quietly asks, "And how do you feel about it?"

Zeke's mouth curls ever so slightly. "It's important that my father lose."

The group nods in agreement as the tension dissipates.

And then the meeting seems to end—or at least, the organized part of the meeting. Two of the men head back to the bar to get refills. The twenty-something starts up a conversation with one of the women, and another leaves in a huff.

A middle-aged woman with her hair held in a bun with two chopsticks leans across the table toward Zeke. "You're okay with this?"

Zeke looks surprised. "Of course. Why wouldn't I be?"

"I mean, it's your family."

He gives her a condescending smile. "In the end, it's what's best for everyone."

"It must be hard for your father?"

Zeke nods. He responds softly with conviction. "Yes, but in the end, he'll lose. It'll take some time for him to come to terms with it, but he'll be okay. My brother, sister, and I will take care of the old man."

"How does your mother feel about it?"

"She died when I was born."

"I'm so sorry."

"It's okay." Zeke leans forward. "She is buried up there, where my dad lives. I think allowing more logging wouldn't be something she'd want. Or maybe she would."

The woman is quiet for a few moments.

Zeke settles back in his seat, watching her. "I know everyone here thinks we're fighting for change, but we're not. We're fighting to prevent change. Those voles would be fine if my father were left up there alone to knock down a few trees every year. Heck, the voles have been there for the last hundred years, and the forest has been logged three or four times."

"Then why aren't we supporting your father?"

"Because of whatever comes next. My father isn't going to live forever. Everyone and everything is circling. His land isn't for sale—until it is."

DONALD KARLSSON MOVES to the witness box. Kent notices the grace with which the old man moves, as though he understands that even in this courtroom, out of his element, he is sure of his place in the world, and no one—not a prosecutor, not a judge, not even a reporter—can change that.

Stacy stands in front of the defendant's table holding a yellow legal pad. She nods to Don, who sits ramrod straight and doesn't nod back. Kent notes she is smiling, trying to get Don to relax, reveal some emotion, show some humanity. Don doesn't flinch.

Stacy clears her throat. "Mr. Karlsson, can you please tell the court where you live?"

Don looks at Judge O'Connell. "36910 Aegolius Creek Highway. End of the road."

"And how long have you lived there?"

"Since I was a teen. Pert near all my life."

Stacy picks up a manila folder and hands its contents to Don. "Is this an accurate representation of your property?"

Don looks at it for a moment before responding, "Yup, that's the homestead. Right there."

Stacy hands the paper to Judge O'Connell. "Your honor, this is a certified Department of Interior map that includes Mr. Karlsson's house and the surrounding area. As you can see, the area around my client's land is overseen by the Forest Service."

Judge O'Connell hands the folder to the bailiff. "Defense Exhibit 1."

Stacy turns back to the witness stand. "Mr. Karlsson, are there trees on your land?"

"Yes."

"And do you want to harvest those trees?"

"Maybe."

Kent notices the judge's eyes widen. Jerry's brow furrows. Why the hell would he file a suit if he wasn't even going to cut down his goddamn trees? What the hell?

Stacy pauses, as if to let the effect of Don's unexpected answer sink in before she continues. "Could you expand?"

"I want the right to be able to log my own trees. I planted them firs when I first settled the property. Before there was a house and such. Well, there's a run-down shack, but not so hospitable, not so you'd call it a house, if you know what I mean. But when I planted them firs there, I decided this was my plot and I was gonna have a real house." Don looks at the courtroom and seems to realize he is rambling. He clears his throat. "Point being, Judge, I thought it was my land and those was my trees, enough so I'd put down roots and plant me a house there right alongside my Doug firs."

Stacy nods her head and moves closer to the witness box. "These are your trees, and you believe that you *own* them. And you want the right to cut them down, even though you may or may not choose to exercise that right."

"Think that's what I just said."

Kent notices Stacy smiling again, trying to soften Don for the judge. He writes furiously. The government is telling a guy who grew his own trees that he can't cut them down. The little guy versus the government mandate. Or maybe the landowner versus the endangered forest. Kent can smell angles, lots of angles to this one. Lots of ways to make it about *the big picture*. He can practically feel the Pulitzer in his hand as he writes.

"What happened on June 18th?"

A furrow appears in Don's brow. For the first time he

appears to show some emotion. "That's when I got the letter." He turns and looks directly at Jerry. "They send me a daggum letter sayin' I can't cut any of my trees on my land because there some daggum critter who lives on 'em."

Stacy picks up the letter from the defense table and hands it to the bailiff. "Here is the letter."

Judge O'Connell reads it and hands it back to the bailiff. "Exhibit 2."

Stacy turns back to Don. "Who gave you the letter?"

"Sheriff Jensen. Drove it all the way up to the house. Said it was straight from the government. Straight from D.C. Said I'd put out for a bid, which was a *damned* lie. A damned lie!"

"So, you were given the letter, telling you not to harvest your trees because there was concern you had asked a logging company for a bid, even though you had not. Is that right?"

Kent wonders why Jerry isn't objecting to what is clearly a leading question. He sees Jerry making notes on a yellow legal pad.

"Yup. Just like I said."

Stacy takes a moment standing at the defendant's table before turning back to the judge.

"Your honor, that's all the questions I have for this witness."

Judge O'Connell turns to Jerry. "Cross?"

Jerry stops scratching on his legal pad and stands up. Kent can tell he's clearly unprepared. "Your honor, we have no questions at this time." It's a mea culpa. He's going to ask for a recess until tomorrow. The first engagement with the opposition was a rout and he knows it. He needs time and a plan.

Kent rushes from the courtroom. For the first time in years, he's excited to start writing.

CHAPTER FIVE

"Treat the earth well: it was not given to you by your parents, it was loaned to you by your children. We do not inherit the Earth from our Ancestors; we borrow it from our Children."

— *CRAZY HORSE*

SEVEN MILES up the Aegolius Highway, the road makes a hard, leftward turn. When a driver—either due to distraction, inebriation, or a suicidal ideation—fails to follow the contours of the road and aims their vehicle straight ahead as the highway veers to the left, they do not plunge from the elevated roadway into a ditch, plow into a tree, or roll their car into a field of livestock. Rather, they feel a gentle drop as they careen, more or less intact, onto an inauspicious, unlined roadway that meanders through the oaks and Doug firs and up the hills on the south side of the valley.

When the distracted driver continues down this hidden roadway a bit further, over a cattle guard and behind a thicket of ponderosa pines, they find an old, rotting barn with a corrugated aluminum roof, a small shack covered in cedar shingles, and a small field fenced with barbed wire.

The farm belongs to Jim Mallet and was bequeathed to him by his father, Jim Sr. The elder Mallet bred horses on the property, small though it was, with the belief that one or two might run at the Portland Raceway. But without the equipment, knowledge, or stock, his hopes never came to fruition, and he died without seeing a single animal on the track. In contrast to his father, Jim Jr., was more pragmatic and prioritized making money over the dream of racing thoroughbreds.

Thus, after coming upon Jim's barn, shack, and field, if the driver were to pause for a moment, they might initially note the odd juxtaposition of the dilapidated barn and shack against the red and white steel fence posts, tied together by several strands of tightly pulled barbed wire, so new its silvery sheen shows no rust.

Though the driver might briefly find the old building and new fence strange, a glance at the foliage scattered throughout the enclosed field or a whiff of its pungent odor would provide nearly instant understanding. For Jim Jr.'s reconstituted farming operation and the crop it produces were, until recently, illegal.

When the hearing resumes, Kent makes sure to sit in the front row, which isn't as easy as it was the day before. The courtroom is now packed. Environmentalists, land rights groups, government officials, and even a few members of the press have decided that U.S. vs. Karlsson is a case worth following. Kent is elated.

Jerry has three assistants sitting with him at the defendant's table. While his suit is immaculate, bags protrude under his eyes, and his hair is slightly disheveled. On the table in front of him are several neatly stacked piles of paper. He is organized, ready.

As Stacy and Don enter the courtroom, a hush falls over the crowd. A man near the back wearing a gray Stetson stands up, reaches out, and shakes Don's hand. A woman in a blue, Earth Defender tee shirt sneers.

When Judge O'Connell enters the courtroom, she waits for the crowd to stand before ascending to the bench. She sits and motions for everyone to do the same. Silently, she looks at the crowd then turns to Jerry. "Are you ready to proceed?"

He stands. "Yes, your honor. The United States calls Dr. Fred Richards to the stand."

A stout man sitting behind the defense table stands and makes his way to the witness box. He is wearing a tweed jacket and reading glasses hung from a lanyard around his neck. As he is being sworn in, Don leans over and whispers to Stacy, who motions to quiet him.

Jerry begins with a series of questions about Richards' professorial qualifications, expertise, and research. Kent notes that Judge O'Connell isn't paying much attention.

Jerry turns to questions about the vole—which, according to Richards, hasn't been given an official name yet. Jerry tries to emphasize that the vole is a newly discovered life form, but his efforts are undermined by Richards' dry, scientific responses.

Then Jerry pauses his questioning. Kent knows that when Jerry pauses, he counts to thirty to ensure it's long enough to get the courtroom's attention. It works. Judge O'Connell looks up. Kent stops doodling. "Professor Richards, why is this animal, this newly discovered creature, considered endangered?"

Richards takes off his glasses and rubs them, looking very much like an emeritus professor of the biological sciences. Kent can tell he has been well prepared. "As far as we know,"

Richards says, "this species exists only in the northeastern area of the Aegolius Creek watershed. Given its limited habitat, any removal of that habitat could end the existence of the species."

Kent writes furiously in his notebook. This question—Why is this animal endangered?—is a pivotal part of the defense's argument. Kent plans to explain to readers, through a series of articles, how the Endangered Species Act of 1973 works. In his first article, he will suggest the editors highlight the following: *a species must be listed as threatened or endangered if there is present or threatened destruction, modification, or curtailment of its habitat or range.* Kent decides Richards's words are the central part of tomorrow's story.

Without so much as a gesture toward the defendant's table, Jerry sits. Stacy waits for a nod from the judge before standing to approach Richards. "Professor, you said the habitat is in the Aegolius Creek Watershed and nowhere else. Is that correct?"

"Yes."

"How do you know?"

"Because that's where we found them."

Stacy brow furrows. "Oh, I see. And where else have you looked?"

Richards looks confused. "Well, nowhere. But...there are lots of wildlife surveys done throughout the forests of western Oregon. And the yet unnamed species has never been identified."

Stacy folds her arms. "The surveys. They happen every year?"

"Most years, yes."

"And they include the Aegolius Creek watershed?"

"Many surveys have, yes."

"And this 'unidentified species' was never noted on these prior surveys?"

Richards shifts in his seat. "No."

Stacy's eyes narrow. "I'll ask you again. Professor, how do

you know the habitat of this species is only in the Aegolius Creek watershed?"

Professor Richards looks at Jerry, whose hands are gripping the arms of his chair so hard his knuckles are white. He looks back at Stacy and starts to stammer before she interrupts. "The correct answer is you don't know." She looks at Judge O'Connell. "I'm done with this witness."

Jerry declines to redirect. Kent tears out the page he had been writing on and crumples it up.

The next morning, Jerry asks for a continuance. Judge O'Connell gives him a week but reminds him of the urgency of the temporary restraining order. Kent has never seen Jerry look so completely and utterly defeated. He asks for an interview as Jerry's assistant exits the courtroom but knows it won't be possible. He's also tried to talk to Stacy and Don, but they won't give him the time of day. Finally, somewhat out of desperation, he begins interviewing courtroom watchers.

Two middle-aged women in jeans and flannel shirts claim to represent organic farmers; they're worried about a ruling affecting their use of land. A large fellow in a rugby shirt says he's hoping the case won't impact the fishing industry. A man wearing a Stetson and black boots declines to talk. But when Kent finds a small group of scruffy, long-haired individuals, he feels like he has a story.

The Forest Militia wants to talk, if not in the most articulate manner. "We will engage in whatever resistance necessary to maintain the integrity of the trees along the Aegolius," notes one young man in a green tee shirt with a frayed collar and a black, knit cap. A woman wearing Birkenstocks and a long skirt says, "It's not right for people to destroy an animal's habitat for greed." When a tall, skinny blond fellow says, "Even the guy's son doesn't want him to cut down the trees," Kent sees the potential for the human element he needs to advance his narrative around *the big picture*.

. . .

Stacy slides into a booth at The Lumberman across from Billy. She glances around at the faux leather booths surrounding the lacquered plywood tables. Once, it was a place where men, and only men, would come to drink and swear and do business, selling lots of land, garnering the best deals for haulers, or picking up a crew, all while imbibing pints of Bud or Henry's. And now, the bar feels old. Old like the wagons at the pioneer museum. Old like the saw blades hanging behind the bar. Old like the men who once crossed the union and made deals with nothing more than a handshake.

"Why aren't you stayin' at the house?" Billy doesn't look up from the laminated menu. He's wearing his work clothes: gray Dickies and a brown jean jacket with "Billy" embroidered on the left pocket. His thick forearms rest on the edge of the table, and his hands are grooved with callouses and stained black by rubber and tar.

Stacy ignores the question. "I can't believe this place is still open."

"Hasn't changed in sixty years."

She picks up the menu. "I'm not staying because it's tiny and depressing."

Billy looks over the top of his menu and frowns. "Depressing? It's where you came from, or have you forgotten?"

Stacy wipes off the front of the menu with a napkin. She knows Billy understands her reluctance to spend a single night in the house where she grew up without a mother. She knows he understands that she avoids the place where the one person who might have helped her through the disappointment of high school dances and school clothes picked out with a father and brothers, where the one person who could have smoothed the sharp edges and disjointed explanations for the changes she went through is buried. And being near

Mother's grave is a reminder of all that. She knows Billy understands, even if he can't articulate or admit it. But still, he asked.

She sets her menu down. "Dad needs to move into town. He's getting old, and he isn't going to last out there much longer."

Billy's eyes narrow. "Why are you helping him stay?"

"I'm not. I'm giving him the ability to use his land as he sees fit. That's not an endorsement of his residence."

"I don't get it. You want him to leave, but you're fighting the government to let him stay."

Before she can answer, a waitress stops at the booth. "Can I get you anything?"

Stacy picks up the oversized laminated menu shaped like the end of a log and turns it over. Every item on the menu includes meat or eggs. Even the hashbrowns are "fried in bacon grease." She orders coffee, black, and Billy orders the Denver omelet. The waitress leaves, oblivious to the familial tension she interrupted.

Stacy sinks back into the faux leather cushion. "I'm going to help Dad. He needs to feel empowered, but that doesn't mean he shouldn't leave. I'll fight for him, but that doesn't mean I want him to stay."

"Sounds like you might want the land for yourself."

Stacy chuckles, shaking her head. "Billy, what the hell would I do with a hundred acres in Oregon? I live in Boston." She leans forward with her arms on the table. "And if I wanted any parcel of land, *that* parcel would literally be the last one I'd want."

The waitress returns with coffee, and Stacy doesn't thank her.

Billy looks across the table. "Dad will never leave. You know that."

"At some point, he won't have a choice."

Billy looks away. "And then what? You gonna keep the place? Give it away?"

"To be honest, I don't care. He decides to sell it, keep it, I couldn't care less."

"When you moved away, I kept thinkin' you were coming back. Thought that for years. Even after you moved back east, I thought it'd be a short spell."

Stacy's eyes bore a hole in his. "You know me as well as anyone. Why would I ever think about coming back?"

They sit quietly for a moment.

A group of men, all wearing hoodies with the same landscaping company logo, enter The Lumberman and loudly make their way to a large booth in the back. They glance at Stacy as they walk by. She wonders if she has changed, if her ability to blend into the establishment's aged decor has waned.

The waitress returns with Billy's omelet. He slowly puts his napkin onto his lap and dumps Tabasco on his plate. Stacy doesn't say a word. She knows he needs a moment to think.

"That land is ours," he finally says between bites. "It belongs to us."

"Actually, it's Dad's. And he will cling to it as long as he can. That accursed place."

"That *place* is where Mom is buried."

Stacy looks at her coffee. She remembers hating the bitter flavor. She'd pour tablespoons of sugar and milk into the black liquid Don made every morning, hoping to mask the taste. Now she drinks it black. She wonders when her habits—when *she*—changed. "My point exactly."

"Well, maybe the rich lawyer in Boston doesn't want it, but maybe I do."

The waitress sets the bill on the table. Stacy picks it up. "I really don't care what happens to the homestead. You can burn it to the ground."

Billy shakes his head. "It's a great place for a farm, after it's logged."

Stacy smirks. "A farm? Are you going to raise some cows? Or hogs? I don't see you as a chicken kind of guy."

"I'm not. I'm gonna log it and start a cannabis operation. That's where the real farming money is these days."

Stacy raises her eyebrows. "Cannabis? Seriously?"

"I'm gonna take the old barn out back and turn it into a greenhouse for the winter months. Wire it up, maybe put in solar panels and run it all night. Jimmy Williams over in Springfield has a dispensary. He says he'll buy from me direct. I get a grower's license from the state, put out a hundred pounds a year, and make six figures." Billy sits back in his seat and folds his arms.

Stacy takes a drink of coffee. "Sounds like you've got quite the plan."

"Damn right. I've seen what the big growers make. I'll make enough to buy the whole damn valley." Billy picks up his fork, takes a final bite of omelet.

"Maybe you want Dad gone."

He frowns. "Of course not. But he's set in his ways and needs to think about the future. About what's comin'. The world's changed. He plans to sit out there until he dies, but I want to move forward."

Stacy pulls a credit card from her handbag and sets it on the bill. Billy pushes his plate back and reaches for his wallet, but she holds up her hand. "The rich Boston lawyer's got this."

He smiles. "For whatever it's worth, you don't look like a rich Boston lawyer. You're still an Oregon girl."

Stacy decides Billy is complimenting her. She's always kept her family at arm's-length from her career, initially out of embarrassment. She vividly remembers them showing up to her law school graduation, hollering and pumping their fists when she walked across the stage, much to the chagrin of the other, mostly upper-middle-class, staid parents. But her embarrassment is coupled with a sense of protection, something inculcated by the death of her mother.

She points at the check as the waitress walks by. "One of the first cases I tried when I started work as a public defender was this guy charged with loitering. He was homeless, living in a box off the Common in front of the Four Seasons. Someone —the hotel or a resident who lived in the expensive, nearby condos—didn't want him there and told the police to remove him. The guy didn't have anywhere else to go, so he moved his box from in front of the hotel to the Common itself." She paused. "Unfortunately, he picked a spot right next to the carousel. And people came unglued. There were other homeless, or maybe I should say houseless, people already living on the Common, but they weren't seen as encroaching on the nice families using the Common Liberal Boston, forged of the revolution, those who decided liberty wasn't as important as their weekends in the park. Somehow that one guy, my client, became the focus of all their ire. They had him arrested, took away his stuff, threw him in jail."

"And you got him off, right?"

"Not exactly. We went through a full jury trial, maybe the only jury trial ever held in Boston on a loitering charge—" Stacy stuffs the bill and her card into the hand of the waitress walking by. "The guy ends up doing time served. He'd been in jail for nearly a month. I appealed the case, but by then, the guy had been paroled and disappeared."

The waitress returns with the bill and Stacy's card. "Justice has very little to do with the law. The law is only a tool, a way to either push toward justice or away from it. It doesn't really matter what the law says—the government will use it to get what they want and call it justice."

Billy looks at the men from the landscaping company. "And that's how you'll get Dad to move."

Stacy nods.

Billy starts to stand. He stops, knees bent as if suddenly frozen and looks directly at Stacy. "You don't intend to win this case, do you?"

She glances at the waitress, who expertly balances four plates while moving toward the table with the landscapers. "We both want Dad to move, don't we?"

Billy drops back into his seat.

Stacy continues. "Getting him to move doesn't require losing the case, but it will help."

He cocks his head. "I'm gonna disagree with you on that one. Dad will never leave that homestead. He'll die there."

Stacy sighs and sets a ten-dollar bill on the table. "Land is just a commodity. Its value rises and falls based on whatever someone thinks it's worth. Nothing more." She touches the money. "No differently than this piece of paper."

"It has a lot of value to Dad."

"Then we'll have to change his perception of its value."

"How are you going to do that?"

Stacy smiles. It's a smile she knows Billy will understand. She smiled the same way whenever she was asked if she liked a certain boy, or if she had a good hand when they played Hearts.

KENT SITS in his cubicle and stares at his computer. He loves and hates the device. The handheld entirety of human knowledge limits the scrolling through microfiche, chatting up the listless personnel at the Department of Records or listening to audio files of untranscribed court proceedings. But it also means anyone can be a journalist. The tools of the craft have become obsolete. All because of the little box sitting on his desk.

When he finally accepted that his skill set had been relegated to the internet, Kent decided his role as a journalist would be defined not by investigation but narration. The narrative, the story, or more precisely, the *telling* of the story would be his calling. Weaving facts into an arch, finding intersects between the story and the reader, exposing the motivations that lurk behind the experts and pundits; these are the skills that Kent now considers central to his profession.

And in the telling of this story, Kent realizes he needs a protagonist. Among the Karlssons, he hasn't yet figured out who that might be. Jerry is the heroic prosecutor, fighting for environmental protection. Old man Karlsson is the steadfast rugged individualist, standing fast against the force of government. He isn't sure about Stacy, but he's intrigued.

The phone in his cubicle buzzes.

CHAPTER SIX

*"The art of our necessities is strange
That can make vile things precious."*

— WILLIAM SHAKESPEARE

After the Aegolius has flushed out the spring rains, when the glories of summer are in full bloom and the days start so early even songbirds are quiet when light warms the morning sky, the big field up yonder underneath the powerlines turns from straw yellow to vivid purple, signaling the arrival of the Aegolius bounty. In the midst of the violet sea, buried in the islands of thorny vines, one can find ripened jewels. For there is no treasure as delightful as the sweet succulent juices of a plump Oregon blackberry.

Like other Aegolius residents, the Oregon blackberry is the progeny of sojourners, stolen away from distant lands, mixed with other immigrant vines, and rooted deep in the volcanic soil. The vines, with their vicious thorns and tiny white flowers, engulf meadows and fields with the voraciousness of wolves consuming a fresh carcass. Every open area in western Oregon is at risk of being occupied by a head-high morass of woody limbs springing up from the ground and woven together in a knot of discordant brambles.

When the vines aren't substantial, they are often tolerated, for as anyone who has tasted a slice of Oregon blackberry pie knows, the vine's harvest provides a delicious compensation for thorn-impaled hands.

Taming the wild vines is left to a small army of goats, raised by exasperated landowners seeking a solution to the amorphous mountains of vines that accumulate nearly anywhere there is adequate sunlight. Goats are the only thing in the Aegolius more rapacious than the Oregon blackberry. The goats are usually tied to a tree or a stake in the ground and diligently, they will mow away whatever vegetation they can reach. After a week or two, the ground has been razed, and all that remains are a few nubbins where the vines used to be.

KENT IS surprised Stacy Karlsson has agreed to meet. In his twenty-eight years of reporting experience, he can recall two or three times an attorney actively involved in a case did so. And figuring out how to reach out to Stacy hadn't been easy, either. Calls to her office, voice mails, pleas to her administrative assistant, even a note passed via the bailiff at the courthouse hadn't seemed to work. Until it did.

He'd almost erased her email without reading it. He expected there to be parameters, things he couldn't ask about. He'd even asked. But there were none.

They agree on a café in Crawfordsville, The Blind Owl. Kent suspects Stacy wants to meet somewhere outside the confines of Portland or Eugene for the sake of privacy. While her picture has been in the local papers, little has been written about her role in the case, other than as Donald Karlsson's attorney.

The Blind Owl is a block from Market Street, also known as Highway 136, between a consignment shop and an empty lot. It's early afternoon, a few minutes after the agreed-upon time. Kent looks for a fancy car outside, something a high-priced lawyer from Boston would drive. Instead, he finds a 1998 Subaru wagon parked next to several pickups and a broken down Jeep.

As he opens the door, Kent sees Stacy sitting in a booth, flipping through a sheath of documents. She is the only customer in the café. She looks plain, and comfortable, as though she belongs in a café in Crawfordsville.

Stacy doesn't look up as Kent approaches her table and stands uncomfortably until she acknowledges him.

"You're late," she says.

"Sorry. I got a bit lost."

Stacy raises her eyebrows. "In Crawfordsville? It has three streets and two stoplights."

Kent tries to change the topic as he sits. "I assume you've been here before."

"Why would you assume that?"

He clears his throat. "Well, I understand you grew up with your dad, up the Aegolius."

Stacy puts the papers she has been reading back in her leather bag. "That doesn't mean I came to Crawfordsville very often, does it?"

"It a reasonable assumption."

A waitress emerges from the back room. She's young, with reddish hair and wearing a faded orange, flannel shirt and jeans. As she approaches, Stacy looks up and smiles. Kent can't tell if they know each other.

They both order black coffee, and Stacy asks, "Don't you have blackberry pie on Thursdays?" The waitress nods, and she asks for a piece.

"I thought you've never been here before?"

"I didn't say that. I asked why you assumed that I had."

Kent pulls out a small notebook and a recorder.

Stacy motions to the machine. "I'll talk to you on background, but I don't want any recordings, and I don't want my name used."

"Are you sure? You're representing the plaintiff. You don't exactly have anything to lose."

"I'm sure." Stacy pulls out her phone. "And I want a verbal assurance."

"My word is usually adequate."

"You're a reporter. I'm willing to talk to you, but on background and only as a confidential source. But if we're going to do this, I need something to hold you accountable." She holds up the phone and taps Record.

"I agree that I will not identify you as the source of any information you impart to me."

Stacy taps again and sets the phone on the table. "Good. Now ask me some questions."

Kent flips the notebook open. "All right. First question. Does your father really intend to cut down the trees on his property and potentially wipe out an endangered species?"

"I don't know."

"Seriously? You have no idea?"

"Seriously. My father may cut them down, and he may not. That's not really the point. What he wants, what he cares about, is his *right* to cut them down."

Kent sighs. She could have told him this on the steps outside the courtroom. "Well, what do you think? Should he have the right to kill off an endangered species?"

"Right now, no one can prove it's endangered."

"What if it is?"

"Then the government can prove it, and the rule of law will apply."

Kent closes his notebook. "Look, if all you're going to do is give me the same answers I'd get in public, there isn't much point in this meeting." He begins to stand. "I'm sorry I've wasted your time."

"Wait." Stacy motions for him to sit. "Yes, I've been here before. During law school, I'd study here on the weekends. I couldn't afford to live in Eugene, so I'd spend weeknights sleeping on friends' couches and go home on the weekends. I'd drive down here because it's quiet and empty." She presses her fingers together. "My dad has cut a handful of trees every year to pay his property taxes, since I can remember. I don't think that will change."

Kent flips the notebook open again. "Okay. And how does the rest of the family feel?"

"That's complicated. I have two brothers. One thinks Dad should be able to cut whatever he wants. The other doesn't."

"And you?"

"I don't care. I'm mostly worried about my father living alone out in the woods without anyone looking after him."

Kent doesn't look up as he jots notes in shorthand. "The daughter on the East Coast feels guilty she can't look after her father and wants him to move somewhere someone else can?"

Stacy is quiet as she looks toward the kitchen. Kent worries she's going to end the interview or throw her coffee at him.

"No," she says. "I mean, maybe. My motivations are beside the point. He's old. He should be closer to other people."

"Don't your brothers live nearby?"

"They do, but I'm not sure they're as concerned as I am."

Kent looks up. "Not feeling as guilty?"

"Perhaps." Stacy looks back at Kent. "When I was sixteen, I couldn't wait to leave that godforsaken place as fast as I could. School was my way out. I studied my ass off to make sure I wouldn't have to come back. I'd visit for holidays, but otherwise, I wouldn't have to think about where I'd come from."

Kent stops writing and puts down the pen. "That must have been hard, coming from a small town and going to the big city."

Stacy picks up a spoon. "When I started college, I didn't know how to hold a spoon correctly." She grasps the utensil in her fist. "I thought you held it like this. I watched the other kids who came from places with money. Middle-class places. I watched, studied, copied them to fit in." She moves her hand to hold the spoon between her index finger, middle finger, and thumb. "Little graces are important. Particularly if you don't know they exist."

"That must have been hard," he says again.

Stacy sets it down. "For a time. But coming from out in the sticks has its advantages as well."

"Tell me about your brothers. William and Ezekiel."

"Billy and Zeke."

"Yes."

The waitress returns with Stacy's pie. "Mom says it's fresh," she says.

"You'd better bring him one, too." Stacy takes a bite and closes her eyes. "Nothing better than Oregon blackberry pie." She opens her eyes. "Billy and Zeke both live in the area. Billy's a lot like my dad. He works as a mechanic. He's rough around the edges but would give you the shirt off his back. After high school, he joined the Army for a couple years, didn't really know what he wanted to do. He assumed a job would be waiting for him at Weyerhaeuser, or in the woods, or somewhere locally. But it never happened. By the time he started looking, the jobs had all dried up. He worked at that Sony factory in Springfield for a while, and in a lot of different places. Got married, then divorced."

"How does he feel about the tree voles?"

"Same as my dad. Billy wants to take over the property when Dad's gone. Obviously, he wants to be able to log it."

"And Zeke?"

Stacy looks toward the windows lining the front of the cafe. "Zeke disagrees."

Kent smells a narrative. "Why?"

"I'm not sure how to put it. Zeke's always had a different relationship with the forest. I wanted to leave. Billy wants to cut it down. And Zeke—well, it's like a spiritual thing for him.

"When we were kids, we'd have to walk about a half mile from where the school bus picked us up and dropped us. In the winter, we'd walk through the woods when it was getting dark. Billy and I hated it. It was scary, you know, being out there alone in the night. We'd run as fast as we could to get home, out of the dark. But Zeke would take his time. We'd get home and then a half-hour later, we'd have to go looking for Zeke. We'd find him sitting somewhere along the road, looking up at the trees." Stacy shook her head. "He said he felt safe out there."

"It sounds like Zeke wants to preserve the forest around your father's homestead because he feels some connection to it?"

"It's more than that. I used to think it was because our mother is buried on the property. He never knew her. She died when he was born." Stacy shakes her head. "Billy and I used to catch crawdads every summer in the creek. We'd take this blue plastic bucket to the edge of the creek and try to fit it with as many as we could. We'd get a couple dozen and take them to Dad, who'd boil them with butter so we could eat the tails. If Billy and I didn't carry the bucket with us the whole time, Zeke would dump it out and let them go."

The waitress returns with a second piece of Oregon blackberry pie. Kent takes a bite and can't believe how good it tastes. He wonders how he's spent so many years in Oregon and never had blackberry pie.

"What kind of work does Zeke do?" he asks.

"He's a librarian at the Eugene Public Library."

Kent sets his fork down and picks up his pen again. "Is this an ideological thing? Do you think he'll try and stop your father from logging?"

Stacy's eyes narrow. "Ideological isn't exactly right. It's more instinctual, like he believes he's got some connection to the Aegolius and has to protect it. I think he recently joined some environmental group."

"And what about your father?"

She shrugs. "What about him? He's been out there by himself for years. He's old and stubborn."

"What did he do? For work?"

"Lots of things. Worked in the woods for many years, then the mill. Odds and ends after the mill closed."

Kent thinks for a moment. He's not sure how to ask the question, so he blurts it out. "Why are you talking to me? What's your motivation?"

"Because I need the story to be told correctly. I need people to know my father isn't up there looking for a Ruby Ridge moment." Stacy leans forward. "And that he may not be well."

"What do you mean, not well?"

"He's forgetful. He loses things. He gets confused easily."

Kent scratches down more notes. "Is he competent?"

Stacy responds. "Define competent. Legally, yes. Functionally, less so."

"Can I meet him?" Kent asks.

"Maybe, but not now. He's a private man. He's lived out there alone for a long time. I'm not sure he'd be open to talking to a reporter."

"I understand." Kent decides it's best to leave the door open a bit. "What's your legal strategy?"

Stacy smiles. "Challenge their claims, force them to admit they're wrong, win the judgment to end the restraining order."

"You make it sound easy."

"In some ways, it is. They don't have the science figured out. At least not yet. And without that, they don't have a case."

Kent nods. "What would you do if you were the feds?"

"Probably the same thing they're doing already. Work on the science as quickly as possible and hope there's enough by the time the judge makes a decision." Stacy pauses for a moment and waits for Kent to stop writing. "Or try to prove he's not of sound mind."

"Do you think they will?"

"I would."

Kent shovels another forkful of pie in his mouth. He wonders for a moment whether it's ethical to write about another man's mental state without having ever met him. But the thought is fleeting, and the pie is delectable.

SHERIFF JENSEN IS skeptical whenever someone hands him a flier and tells him a protest is imminent. Skeptical because conservative Linn County isn't exactly a hotbed of radicalism. The last violent protest Jensen remembers was during the '80s when the mill workers' union went on strike and tried to overturn a bus full of replacement workers. After sticking the union leaders into a cramped holding cell and turning off the heat for a night, the protest quieted, and a settlement was quickly reached—which Jensen regards as proof his method was effective. Since then, he hasn't been concerned about protests.

Which is why he crumples up the flier Deputy Jim Livingston has placed on his desk and round files it with little more than a thought.

Jim shakes his head. "Don't think that's important?"

Jensen sits in the roller chair behind his desk. "No, I do not."

"Says there's going to be a protest up by the Karlsson ranch."

Jensen leans back in the roller chair. "When was the last time you saw a timber protest?"

Livingston scratches his nose. "I 'member Dick tellin' me about one in Oakridge a few years back."

Jensen tips his hat. "That was a decade ago. It lasted all of a week. And it was on public land."

Livingston nods. "So, no protest then?"

Jensen smiles. "No protest."

CHAPTER SEVEN

"A soft answer turneth away wrath: but grievous words stir up anger. The tongue of the wise useth knowledge aright: but the mouth of fools poureth out."

— PROVERBS 15:1-2

IN THE FARTHEST reaches of the Aegolius Valley, near where the valley walls become sheer and the basalt cliffs are laced with volcanic soils, there is a hole in the ground. Described by some as a cave, said to be ill-suited for spelunking or underground exploration—though just how difficult it is to traverse varies widely depending on the source of the information. Whether large enough to accommodate a wayward hunter seeking shelter from an autumn storm, or the sort of cavernous space best suited for a bear's hibernation, local lore insists it could either be a large, volcanic tube or barely more than a small crevasse.

In either case, the Indian Head Cave is a source of mystic interpretation. For, as the name implies, it contains an aged, human skull, reportedly from one of the valley's earliest inhabitants. Nothing definitive exists to ascribe the origin of the skull, and to whom it belonged provides a never-ending source of speculation and rumor. Was it a native warrior wounded in battle? A hunter mauled by a bear? An instrument of some ancient rite? Residents less enthralled by the mystical certainty of the skull's origin point out it might as easily be the head of an early settler—perhaps a wayward pioneer or a modern hiker sheltering from a storm.

The hushed tones with which the residents of the Aegolius describe Indian Head Cave reveal a certain reverence for its occupant. Regardless of identity, the remains are tied to the valley, their spirit interred within the rocks and the soil and the trees. At Aegolius Elementary, the origins of Indian Head Cave are told as ghost stories. The same children's parents, in contrast, focus on the symbolism of human remains buried in the heart of the valley. But perhaps the most intriguing aspect of Indian Head Cave isn't the manner in which it's described, but the nature of its attribution.

While residents of the Aegolius Valley talk of the Indian Head Cave with an air of certain conjecture, finding someone who has been there is remarkably difficult. Those rendering descriptions invariably start with "my cousin told me" or "his girlfriend's brother said" or "I heard from someone." The few who chase down the enigmatic cousin, girlfriend's brother, or someone to verify the description's source are left with little more than another secondhand story. And the rare, intrepid souls who attempt to find the cave based on the second, third, and fourth-hand accounts are always left disappointed. For when they wander out into the Aegolius forest in search of the cave, they return unsatisfied, asking whether the mystic cave is too well hidden, or buried beneath a landslide, or in some other part of the valley. And for the briefest of moments, they wonder if the cave really is the landmark that all the conjecture, recital, and lore suggests. Or whether it ever existed at all.

. . .

Don steps out on the porch and sees Zeke's Subaru in the drive, empty. He's surprised he didn't hear it drive up. He pulls his suspenders over his shoulders, slips on a pair of old shoes, and begins making his way up the trail behind the house next to the creek. As he nears the little waterfall in the clearing with Marle's headstone, he sees Zeke sitting cross-legged on the ground. For a brief moment, Don sees Marle, sitting and staring at her own headstone, her hair pulled back in a black ponytail offset by alabaster skin. He stops, deciding whether he should say something. He clears his throat.

Without turning around, Zeke speaks in a voice that quietly reverberates across the clearing. "Hey, Dad. Didn't think I'd see you out here—with all that's going on." He looks up. "I needed to talk to you, and Mom."

Don puts his hand on Zeke's shoulder. "She'd like that."

For some time, both men are silent, listening to the forest around them. They listen to the creek rush over rocks and splash to the pool below. To drops of water falling from the moss clinging to the sides of the trees. To the breeze rustling the branches. To the sound of their own breathing.

And they stare at the headstone.

Zeke sighs. "You know she'd never want you to cut down the trees you planted."

"I know. But she'd make sure you kids could if you needed to."

Zeke stands and brushes off his hands. "I'm not sure we'd want to cut them down, either."

Don pats his arm. "Maybe you think that now, but the day may come when you do. They're just trees, Zeke. I planted them to make sure you all had somethin' when I was dead and gone. Somethin' that could be yours. I don't want anybody takin' them away. See, they may be just trees, but they're more than that." His shoulders relax. "When you get to an age, something inside you starts wonderin' what it's all for. Why am I here, and what's gonna be left of me when I'm gone? And you start thinkin' less about the now and more about the then, and you start lookin' to leave things behind. I planted those trees and growed them up, like you and Billy and Stace. And nobody should be able to take 'em away."

Zeke is quiet for a moment then smiles. "They're part of the forest too, Dad. Those trees are connected to you, to me, to Mom, to all of us. You love this place. I don't ever want anyone to destroy any part of it. But it's bigger than us. Trees were here for millions of years before we got here, and there will be trees after we're gone."

"But these are mine. Like I said, they ain't just trees."

"I know, Dad. Which is why I'm going to make sure no one cuts them down."

Don folds his arms. His eyes narrow slightly. "You gonna fight me on this."

He nods. "You know it's only 'cause I love you."

Don reaches down and touches the ground. "You got your mom in you. She used to tell me whenever I'd go to butcher a cow or cut down a tree, I was doin' something that couldn't be undone. She'd tell me it was my job to take what was needed and her job to stop me when it was too much. You're like her in that way. Always remindin' me when it's too much."

"If it's about the money, we'll take care of it."

"It has nothing to do with money."

"Then why fight?"

Don stands. "It's about the principle. Do I get to control my own land? My own forest? I planted those trees. Damn near all of 'em. They're mine to cut. Ain't no man in a suit able to tell me what I can and can't do. If they can take that from me, who's to say they can't take it from you? It ain't about takin' too much, it's about takin' anything at all. Even your mother wouldn't put up with that. That's the thing you got to see, son."

"What if you win? Will you cut?"

"I dunno. Might. Might not." He shrugs. "Billy thinks he's goin' to inherit the place, and Stace wants to stand up to a bully. I want what's mine to be mine."

"What can I do to stop you from cutting?"

"Not sure you can."

"Dad, it's wrong." Zeke stands and grips Don's arm. "I'm not letting you be the man who ends a species to prove a point."

Don pulls his arm away. "It ain't a species, and I ain't endin' it. And them trees are mine to cut. I planted 'em, I own 'em, and I'm gonna harvest 'em whenever I want to."

Zeke nods and without a word, he turns and walks back to his car.

THERE'S A STORY I tell myself. It's about a feller working on a piece of land out in the middle of nowhere. Treats the land good. Takes care of it. Takes only what he needs from it and leaves the rest. Protects it. Then along comes the big ol' government. Men in suits and ties. Men with papers. And they tell that feller he don't get to do what he's been doin' all these years. The feller pushes back, tries to stop 'em from tellin' him what he can and can't do, 'cause he ain't doin' nothing wrong, see. Being a good steward of the place. Like God said to do, he's doin' it. And the government people, they're just wrong.

But then there's another story I tell myself. 'Bout how this guy's got somethin' on his property that's unique. A one-in-the-world kind of thing. He don't think it's such, but he don't really know. And the thing he's doing, the thing he's always done, may make that one-in-the-world critter go away for good. People all around, they're tryin' to stop him, to reason with him, to say, "Hey look at what's happenin'," but he don't want to listen 'cause he thinks they're all wrong.

Which story's right? Am I the hero or the villain? And that's the hard part, see. The villain is the only one who don't know that he's the bad guy. If I am the villain, just by the way of things, I ain't ever gonna know.

STACY DOESN'T USUALLY HEAR answers that surprise her. But her cross-examination of Richards has left her with one she can't escape. The words are so unexpected she repeats them.

"Professor, did you just say, 'Those trees aren't supposed to be growing there'?"

Richards nods. "Yes."

"So, you're saying the trees my client intends to cut down shouldn't be there in the first place?"

He nods again.

Stacy can feel Jerry shifting in his leatherbound chair at the table behind her. She wasn't surprised when he spent three hours in redirect, necessitating a second round of cross-examination. To seasoned court observers, a lengthy second round of questions by either the plaintiff or defendant is a sign of amateurish lawyering. A perception that isn't lost on Jerry.

Once the court was called back into session, Stacy assumed after drubbing Richards once, Jerry would accede, and the judge would ask for closing arguments. Then, he'd present some kind of compromise ruling, one that couldn't be overturned on appeal but wouldn't identify a clear winner. She'd hoped the ruling would require Don to abstain from logging and advise the government to compensate him, but even if it didn't, the case would drag on. If the judge handed the feds a victory, Don would ask Stacy to fight on and, in a scenario that seemed more and more likely, if the judge ruled Don could continue to log, Jerry would push for an appeal. Intransigence is a characteristic not simply confined to her father.

In either case, the judge would let the restraining order stand until the appeal process resolved the matter, and Stacy would let Don know how many years it would take to resolve the matter. He'd be better off selling the lot to someone who could wait it out, she'd say, and wouldn't it be nice to have a place closer to town?

Stacy expected her last foray into court with Jerry to be the end of the matter, but here she is again. Surprised by an answer.

"If that's the case, Professor Richards, why shouldn't my client be able to log the trees on his property? If they aren't supposed to be there, what's wrong with removing them?"

Richards shakes his head. "That's not what I meant."

Stacy is quiet for a moment. "Not what I meant" is normally the kind of phrase she can't hear enough in a trial. It can easily be inferred to mean "what I meant but was trying really hard not to say." It is a wonderful irony for an attorney that judges and juries often find inspired meaning in "not what I meant."

"What did you mean, Professor?"

Richards clears his throat. "A forest composed primarily of Douglas firs isn't a natural phenomenon. Native forests in this area should be a mixture of trees, alder, hemlock, madronas, oaks, cedar, and some Doug firs. But not firs alone. The native forest in that area has been logged at least once, maybe twice, over the last century and replaced by Douglas fir trees. Only Douglas firs. That's what I meant when I said they don't belong there."

"Well then, Professor, if the trees don't belong there, why not cut them down? Give the native forest an opportunity to regrow. If something doesn't belong, why not remove it?"

Again, Stacy can hear uncomfortable shifting at the prosecutor's table. She doesn't smile and works to suppress any hint of schadenfreude.

"Because there is a species in those trees we know little about. Maybe it evolved in response to the overabundance of Doug firs, maybe it was there beforehand—we don't know. If the forest is cut, well, then the western tree vole might become extinct."

Stacy turns back to her legal pad, pretending to write something. She knows she has violated a cardinal rule in court: never ask a question to which the answer isn't already known.

"So, you don't know whether this vole is indigenous or not, do you?"

"No. Which is why we need the trees to stay."

"And how long will that take?"

Richards doesn't respond. It's an opening. Stacy waits. Let observers fill in the gaps.

Then, as he opens his mouth, she speaks. "You really have no idea how long it will take, do you, Professor?"

"No."

"And it may take a very, very long time. Many years even. Isn't that right, Professor?"

"Yes."

"Do you know how old my client is?"

Richards looks at Don Karlsson. "No."

"He's eighty-three. Will he still be alive when you finally figure out whether the trees can be cut down or not?"

Richards starts to mumble an answer, but Stacy cuts him off. "Don't answer that. No more questions."

The Green Tortoise is alive. Alive with the moral imperative of people who are partially inebriated and generally uninterested in questioning the logic of their collective outrage. A crowd gathers in the main bar, standing around a group of tables in the middle of the room. It's an eclectic group, a handful of younger people who might belong at one of the local universities, several middle-aged men and women in professional dress, and a few aged, counterculture types.

A man in a dark blue hoodie stands on a barstool and signals for the crowd to quiet. A hush falls as he begins to speak. "It's a travesty, what's coming. Industry has once again put profits over the environment. They have decided their margins are more important than preserving what little forest we have left. Today in court, their high-powered, East Coast attorney ran roughshod over the protections we the people have created in order to preserve what is in our common good. The court may not have ruled yet, but we know what that ruling is going to be. The game is rigged. Timber barons have the money and the power. They will try to vanquish one of God's creatures from the face of the earth for the sake of the almighty dollar." He pauses and looks around the room. "The question for us now, today, is how will we respond? How will we protect the future? What will we sacrifice for our future, for our children's future?"

A middle-aged man wearing loafers and a blazer blurts out, "We will stop them!" The crowd signals its agreement.

A twenty-something with braids and a silhouette of Che Guevara on her tee shirt raises a fist. "We fucking destroy the machine!" The older members of the crowd appear minimally enthusiastic as they endorse her statement.

The man on the barstool raises his hands again. "Remember Fall Creek! We have done this before. We know how to stop logging and shut down these operations. We know what to do."

A man in a flannel shirt and Birkenstocks shouts, "Remember the Easter Massacre!" It's clear from the crowd's lackluster response they do not.

"We are going to fight this. But to fight we need to organize." The man in the blue hoodie points to a pair of young women near the front. "Jonie and Melissa will take your names. There are a series of actions we'll coordinate, starting with putting people in place to make sure they witness whatever goes down."

The crowd murmurs with approval, and Jonie and Melissa start to circulate and write down names.

As he starts to step down from the barstool, a loud voice emanates from a booth in the back. "And what will you tell the people who need to cut the trees?" The crowd quiets as heads turn.

Zeke asks the question again. "What will you tell the people who need to cut those trees to keep their homes, feed their children, and pay their taxes? What will you tell them?"

The room is silent.

The man in the blue hoodie finally speaks. "We stop them from cutting. What happens after isn't our problem."

A voice from the crowd pipes up. "The trees are what matters."

Zeke's expression doesn't change. "And the people don't?"

The room remains silent for a moment, until the crowd begins to talk in murmurs as though no one has said anything at all.

ZEKE SEES BILLY sitting at the bar when he enters The Timberman. Billy's hand engulfs the pint glass he's nearly finished. The bar is dark. Men in flannel shirts with suspenders and baseball caps sit around the bar and in a few of the booths.

Billy waves Zeke toward a booth and signals the bartender. He stands up and gives Zeke a hug. The brothers are the same height, though Billy's wide shoulders and short cropped hair make him appear taller. Both men have the same black hair, but Billy's skin is ruddy, while Zeke's is smooth and mostly unblemished. "Well, there he is. How you been, little brother?"

Zeke smiles like a Cheshire cat. He doesn't flinch at being

provocatively labeled 'little brother.' "I'm good, Billy. I'm good."

They sit. Billy grins. "How's things in town? You still over at the U?"

Zeke's face doesn't change. He looks serene, unconflicted. "Yup. Still living with some friends."

"Still workin' at the hippie mart?" Billy lightly punches Zeke's shoulder.

"Yup, still at the library."

Billy nods, watching his brother and trying to get a sense of his disposition. But Zeke is a closed book. Always has been. He can't remember a time when he could read Zeke's feelings, even after sufficient goading and prodding.

"Well, you heard about what they're tryin' to do to Dad, right? Make it so he can't cut down his own goddamned trees. Can you believe that? Man doesn't have any power over his own trees. I mean, what's this country coming to if a man doesn't own the thing he owns? Goddamned terrible. Right?"

Zeke sits back and looks Billy in the eye. "Dad doesn't need to cut those trees."

"Well, no, he doesn't need to, but that's not the point. What if he just wants to? Ain't right when a man can't cut down his own trees."

Zeke looks away. "What about those voles that live in them? Might be the only colony of them anywhere in the world."

Billy takes a long drink. He taps his fingers on the table, wondering if he ever understood Zeke. He remembers working hard, splitting wood and cleaning the barn, while Zeke played in the yard. He remembers feeling both protective and jealous, more like a parent than a sibling.

"You and I know those voles have been there a long time. Hell, we shot BB guns at them. Shit, they're just voles."

"And they don't have a right to exist?"

"Fuck no! They don't have no rights! They're goddamned voles!"

Zeke's face softens. "We live in nature's wake, Billy. We live in its wake."

"What the fuck does that even mean?"

The two men sit in silence and drink their beer. Both can feel the invisible wall between them.

"I guess this means you're not gonna support dad." Billy looks back at the bar as he says it.

"This isn't about supporting Dad."

"Then what the fuck is it? The way I see it, we stand up for Dad. Simple. You've always made everything complicated."

Zeke blinks. "It's about something bigger, Billy. Bigger than you and me and Stace and Dad. It's about who we are." He sets the glass down. "You know how you walk through a patch of poison oak, and you break out in a rash? So you get some gloves and try and pull it all out, make a big pile, and light it on fire?"

Billy nods.

"But the worst rash you can get, the one that takes forever to go away and itches through your skin all the way down to your bones, is the one you get when you step into the smoke from the pile of poison oak you set on fire." Zeke's penetrating gaze settles on Billy. "This conflict has already laced the ground with poison. Cutting even one of those trees will be putting a match to it all."

For a moment, the invisible wall comes down. But then Billy sees Zeke, the way he looked when Billy was supposed to protect him, smaller and lost, but with the stubborn glint in his eye. The way he was when he reminded Billy of their mother. Then the wall rises again.

Billy laughs. "Bullshit. You know it's a bunch of bullshit. Those voles are just voles. Nothin' special. And a man can't cut his trees because someone else says they're special." He downs the last of his pint and slams his glass on the table. "You do what you think is right, Zeke. But know you're takin' something away from Dad. Something that's his, something he needs. And it ain't right."

THE RAIN DRIZZLES DOWN as Jensen makes his way back up the Aegolius. Two deputies should have been enough, but the urgency in their voices suggested he might have been wrong.

The number of cars and trucks lining the highway near the Karlsson driveway stretches a quarter mile, maybe more. Jensen drives directly down the middle of the road, lights on. He sees his two deputies standing at the edge of Karlsson's drive. On the highway a small but active crowd yells and chants. Behind the deputies are eight or nine rugged-looking men. Unlike the chanting crowd, they are stone-faced, and armed. Jensen can see at least three holstered pistols and an AR-15 slung over a shoulder. The men look tense. Jensen's deputies, on the other hand, look scared.

Jensen steps out of the Blazer and walks toward his deputies, who look relieved to see him.

"Sheriff, we need help. I think there's goin' be a riot."

Jensen pats his shoulder. "No riots today. Just folks expressing their opinions." He walks past him toward the men with guns.

"Gentlemen. Nice to see you out here today." He realizes he doesn't recognize any of them.

A middle-aged man with black sunglasses and a camo jacket nods. "We're here to uphold Don Karlsson's constitutional rights."

Jensen takes off his hat. "And which constitutional right are you all worried about?"

A shorter, meaner-looking fellow in a baseball hat says, "Man's right to do what he wants with his property."

Jensen nods thoughtfully. "Yup. That's important." He rubs the rim of his hat. The felt on the brim is worn. "By the way, which article of the Constitution is that?"

The men with guns look confused.

He smiles and puts his hat back on. "Oh well, I'm sure it's in there somewhere. Now, here's the thing." He points at the protesters on the highway. "Those folks are expressing their constitutional rights as well. That right would be the First Amendment if you care to look it up. And I'm going to make sure they stay on their side of the property line. What I need you fellas to do is not threaten, provoke, or in any way undermine those folks' constitutional rights." He looks each man in the eye, even the ones wearing sunglasses. Then, without another word, he turns and walks toward the crowd.

One of the deputies has a bullhorn, which Jensen takes as he passes by. He pushes his hat back a bit on his head and holds up a hand. "All right, now. If you folks don't mind, give me a minute." One young man holds up his middle finger, which Jensen ignores. A woman who looks like she should be teaching Sunday school screams something about "going to fucking hell," which Jensen also pretends he doesn't notice. But mostly, the crowd quiets. Jensen talks into the bullhorn. "Look, folks. I know you all have concerns and strong opinions, and want to express your feelings. I'm here to ensure your right to do so is uninfringed. But here's the thing; the owners of that property have rights as well. And if you try to take away their rights, I'll have to arrest you."

A man in a jean jacket yells, "What about them? They've got guns."

Jensen shakes his head. "The property owner has given his permission for those men to be there. And they have a right to carry guns. That would be the Second Amendment." He pauses, considering whether he should note that shooting someone was not constitutionally protected, before concluding that leaving the matter to conjecture might minimize any untoward behavior.

He hands the bullhorn back to the deputy, who looks far less worried than a few minutes before.

As Jensen walks back toward his Blazer, he hears the unmistakable roar of a chainsaw. He freezes. The roar continues, echoing off the trees that line the Karlsson drive.

The crowd becomes silent, listening intently. The deputies and the men on Karlsson's property have all turned to look toward the sound. After a few minutes, the rise and fall of the chainsaw roar gives way to an idle—a low crack followed by creaks and groans. From the highway, the crowd watches as the top of one of the trees further up the drive disappears and crashes to the ground.

It takes a moment for the crowd to realize what has happened. There are quiet gasps before pandemonium ensues.

Jensen runs toward his deputies, who now face a hostile, surging crowd. The men with guns take a few steps back and draw their weapons. Individuals from the crowd break free and move down the Karlsson driveway. Several people start throwing rocks. Jensen hears the pop of an AR-15 and pulls his revolver from its holster. He doesn't see anyone fall to the ground. A warning shot most likely. Hopefully.

As Jensen turns to tell his deputies to call for backup, a sharp pain jolts through his head. As he falls to the ground, he hears more gunfire. And then things go dark.

WHEN HE WAKES UP, the first thing Jensen notices is the color of a nurse's scrubs—the same color worn by inmates in the county jail. For a moment, he isn't certain why he's been thrown into lockup, but his fear subsides when he sees the stethoscope around her neck.

He tries to sit up in bed. It's painful, and he's dizzy after he sinks back into the bed. The nurse checks his vital signs and asks him to track her finger with his eyes. When he's done, she writes something on a slip of paper and leaves the room.

Within moments, Deputy Jim Livingston enters the room. "How you doin', boss?"

"My head hurts."

Livingston takes off his hat and sits on the edge of the bed. "You took a mighty good shot."

Jensen touches his head for the first time. He feels the stitches over his left temple. "A bullet?"

"Nope. Just a rock."

"Can't believe I was taken out by a goddammed rock."

Livingston chuckles. "It was a big rock if that makes you feel any better."

"What happened?"

Livingston's face smooths out. "It was bad. Tipman and Reynolds called for help the minute you went down. Damn near every car made a beeline to your position—including the state police—but by the time we arrived, the riot was basically over. Mostly rocks and shots fired into the air. Some pushing and shoving. Then you got hit, they all stopped."

Jensen closes his eyes. Should have been preventable with just a few more deputies. Should have been goddamned preventable. "How many injured?"

"None. Fortunately, neither side could hit a barn door," Livingston pauses. "'Cept for you. Whoever threw that had good aim."

The nurse returns with a paper cup and two blue pills and puts them in Jensen's hand. He looks down. "What're these for?"

"Your blood pressure. It's much too high."

Jensen looks at the pills, wondering if they'll be enough. He tries to throw his head back as he takes them, but it's too painful. The nurse gives him a cup of water. He puts the pills on his tongue, takes a gulp of water, and swallows. He looks at Livingston. "Arrest him."

"Who?"

"Karlsson. Don Karlsson."

Livingston's eyes widen. "On what charge?"

"Inciting a riot."

"But Don Karlsson wasn't even there. How did he incite the riot?"

"He cut down a tree."

Livingston looks confused. "I don't think the DA will charge him for simply cutting down a tree on his own land."

Jensen pulls himself up in bed, wincing at the pain and wondering how many more blood pressure pills he is going to need. "Charge him. He knew exactly what he was doing. And if you don't want to charge him with inciting a riot, charge him with violating a court order. Or menacing. Or attempting to kill off an endangered species. Or whatever the hell else you can think of. Just charge him. Put him in handcuffs, book him, and throw him in jail."

Livingston doesn't move.

"Now!"

Jensen wonders where the nurse went. His head hurts, and he wants pain medication.

CHAPTER EIGHT

"Who, being innocent, ever perished? And where were upright people ever destroyed? Even as I have seen those who plow iniquity and those who sow trouble reap the same."

— JOB 4:7-8

THE OLD SHAKE mill sits atop the ridge that cascades from the Aegolius hills down to the creek at the entrance of the valley. A two-story tin shack, the lower level is open on one side and covers a large band saw and splitter run by the same, nine-horse gas engine. The teeth of the bandsaw are tinged with rust, which matches the aluminum siding. Hydraulic fluid stains the barrel on the back of the splitter, around which a pile of wood chips and broken bits of shingles slowly rot. The shack's upper floor is accessed by a ladder and contains little more than a desk once piled high with unpaid invoices and unfilled orders. It's dank and cold, as the wind howls through the single, broken window at one end of the room. Pieces of a broken coffee cup sit in a corner as though someone had thrown it against the wall and simply left it there.

The ground outside the shake mill is covered by several inches of sawdust and bits of wood, slowly turning into a dark mush absorbed by the soil below, beginning the process that over enough eons will convert it into coal or oil or some other fossilized energy. One day, a geologist might wonder why their calculations hadn't identified the rich vein right where the shake mill once stood, or how such a vast accumulation of carbon came to be in one place.

That might be what comes of the mill. But today, the faint scent of cedar, tinged with fir, permeates in a manner that attracts deer, wild turkeys, and the occasional fox. The animals wander in and out of the small building, and around a pile of fir rounds leaning against one wall.

No one up the Aegolius quite remembers who owns the mill. They don't recall exactly when it was abandoned, though it must have happened sometime in the mid-1990s when building codes banned the use of wood shakes on roofs, and cedar logs became harder and harder to find. In either case, whoever owned the mill simply walked away, leaving the saw, the splitter, the rounds, and the ladder as if they intended to come back to work the next day.

At first glance, the shake mill might seem a blight, a tin can rising from the pristine forest, a piece of waste tossed into a garden of fir, oak, and madrona. On more careful inspection, the mill appears well-suited to its surroundings, like a fallen tree broken after the winter or the carcass of a deer succumbed to injury or age. Like all things in the Aegolius, it is a reminder of illusory permanence, and that even the deepest roots are ephemeral. Everything ends, sometimes with little more than an exhaled breath.

Two POLICE CRUISERS and a Blazer make their way up the Aegolius Highway. They drive at precisely the speed limit, flashers off. When they reach the Karlsson driveway one of the cruisers stops and turns to block the entrance as the other vehicle rolls up the narrow gravel road.

At the front of the little house, Tim Redborn and another deputy step out of the Blazer.

That's when I see them lawmen for the first time. Serious lookin' fellas. When one shows up, he's there for a talk. When it's more than one, it's certain they're takin' someone with 'em when they leave.

Redborn strides toward the front door, but before he gets there, Don Karlsson steps out onto the porch. Karlsson is imposing, even though he's older and a couple inches shorter than Redborn.

"Don Karlsson?"

The older man doesn't respond.

"You're under arrest for inciting a riot."

At first, I don't know what the heck he's goin' on about.

Karlsson's back straightens. "Weren't no riot here. Just a bunch of angry tree huggers and some friends of Billy's to mind the property."

Redborn holds up a piece of paper. "From the court's perspective, there was. We have a warrant for your arrest. I need you to come and put your hands on the car."

Then it dawns on me. This ain't 'bout the riot, or the protest or whatnot. Them deputies are here 'cause their boss got hit in the noggin'.

Karlsson motions at the paper. "What's it say I did?"

"It says you incited a riot." Redborn motions toward the cruiser again.

Karlsson slowly walks forward and flattens his hands on the car. Without a word, Redborn cuffs him and helps him into the backseat.

The police drive away, with the front door of the little house still open.

I think to myself, this is how government justice works. It's supposed to be blind and all, but really it ain't. The motives of men are always the same, and justice ain't nothin' more than a different way to get what they think they're owed. Greed, lust, avarice, and revenge. It's all the same. Don't matter who's wearin' the badge or poundin' the gavel. In the end, if they want you, they'll be comin'.

KENT IMMEDIATELY NOTES the smell of rubber when he enters Nathan's Tires. It's a noxious smell that leaves him feeling dirty, like the black residue left on one's hands when the Goodyears and Firestones are hauled off the racks that line the walls of the small warehouse.

As he enters the office, he steps to the counter and asks if Billy is working. The short, ponytailed woman behind the counter points through a large window to the attached garage and a series of bays, where he can see vehicles sequentially hoisted, their tires removed, repaired, or replaced, set back on the garage floor, and driven away. One or two men in each bay scurry about as the ripping sound of lug nut drills untethering tires echoes off the walls with deafening ferocity. Most of the men wear jumpsuits, steel-toed boots, and black work gloves. They appear indifferent to the sound, the smell, and each other. Kent is reminded of the inside of a beehive where drones and workers move through a sequence of behaviors, so completely engrained by evolutionary selection they barely notice what they are doing.

He exits the office and makes his way to Bay 6, where he sees Billy, ripping lug nuts off a small, Nissan pickup. Billy is wearing blue coveralls, and his ears are covered by black industrial earmuffs. His height is accentuated by the rigidity of his back and his dark brown hair, cut short and a bit thin on top. Even under the coveralls, his lean musculature is apparent.

Kent waves to get his attention.

Billy stops, pulls off his earmuffs. "What?"

"I'm a reporter from *The Oregonian*. I'm wondering if we can talk?"

He shakes his head. "What?"

"I'm a reporter. I'm…" Billy sets down the drill and takes a step towards Kent.

Kent raises his voice. "I'm a reporter. I'm here to—"

Billy puts up a hand. "I'm not talking to anyone from the press." He turns away.

Kent, not sure if he should continue to shout, lest he appear too aggressive, responds. "I've already talked to Stacy."

Billy stops. "You talked to my sister?"

"Yup."

"What'd she say?"

"We talked about your dad. About your upbringing. I'm working on a profile of your family."

Billy looks at Kent, who immediately feels the same, penetrating gaze he received from Don. "All right. I'll talk. But only 'cause Stace did." He pulls off his gloves, sets them on a bench, and then motions for Kent to follow.

Behind the shop, Billy pulls out a vape pen and draws a slow breath.

Kent waits for him to exhale before speaking. "Thanks for talking with me. I'm trying to put together a piece about your family—how everyone feels about the injunction, what you're all planning to do, that sort of thing."

Billy leans against the building. "I think we're against it. Takes Dad's rights away."

"What do you think the government should do about the tree voles?"

"They can do whatever they want. But you can't prevent a man from doing what he wants on his own property. That's plain wrong."

Kent pulls out a small notepad from his back pocket. The first questions are always conversation openers, something to start them talking. He already knows what the answers will be, but getting people to open up is as much a science as an art, and countless attempts have taught him to start with obvious questions.

"What do you think your father will do if the injunction is granted?"

Billy shrugs. "Not sure. He might obey the order. Then again, he might ignore it." He looks away for a moment before continuing. "Dad isn't a real 'people person.' He's been up there all alone since Mom died and we kids left. Doesn't have any real friends to speak of, or any extended family that comes by. It's just him. Him and the trees."

"Do you think he'd risk going to jail?"

"He might."

Kent scratches in his notebook. "What about you?"

"What about me?"

"Tell me about yourself. I read some information about your background online but want to get to know the real you."

Billy straightens up. "What did you find online?"

"Just public records. You graduated from Crawfordsville High. Married and divorced. No kids. Stuff like that."

Billy nods, his eyes wary.

"How long have you worked here?" Kent asks.

"Six, maybe seven years. Started right after Jen and I split up."

"Do you like it?"

"It's all right. The manager's a friend, and it pays the bills."

Kent looks at the area behind the building. A chain link fence supports stacks of used tires. The area is dirty, covered with bits of rubber, rusted car parts, and garbage.

"Are you worried about your father?"

Billy chuckles. "My old man is as tough as the trees around his house. He's like an old, gnarled root. Ain't no one going to pull him off his place."

"What do you see happening if they do?"

"Not sure. Someone will have to take over for him. I'll probably end up moving out there."

Kent continues to scribble in his notebook. "Tell me about your mother."

"Died when Zeke was born. Bled out, I was told." Billy pulls out his pen and takes another drag. "She's still buried up there, you know."

"So I've heard. Tell me about your brother Zeke. Does he feel differently about your situation?"

Billy looks at the notebook on the table and shakes his head. He thinks for a moment before responding. "Zeke's complicated."

"What do you mean?"

"Some people want to own land; some people feel like they're a part of it."

"And Zeke?"

"Have you seen it?"

Kent stops writing. "What?"

"The land. The property. What we're talkin' about. Have you seen it?"

"Not yet, no."

Billy looks around as though he doesn't want to be overheard. "When we was kids, Dad made us go to Sunday school. I hated it. Used to mess around with my friends and cause trouble all the time. Stace liked it at first, but after a while, she'd hide a book inside her Bible so she could read something else. Zeke, on the other hand, always was taken by it. When we were twelve or thirteen he stopped wearing shoes outside. Just stopped. Didn't matter how cold it was or if he was going to have to walk on gravel or anything."

"Why? And what does that have to do with Sunday school? Or your dad's property, for that matter?"

Billy clears his throat. "Remove the sandals from your feet, for you stand upon holy ground. It's from somewhere in Acts, I think Zeke took that to heart. Did it for a couple years, whenever he went outside." Billy pauses and looks around again. "That's Zeke. He believes the property around the house is some kind of holy ground and shouldn't be touched."

Kent nods and then starts writing again. Then he looks up. "And what about you?"

"There ain't nothin' holy about that land, or any land. In the end, it's only worth whatever it's got on it, or under it. The most valuable thing about the homestead is the trees, and the spring that runs through it."

The Linn County Adult Corrections facility is located directly across the street from Farmer's Union Coffee. On summer mornings when the wind comes from the south, the scent of roasting arabica beans permeates the orange brick with an intensity that makes everyone within know morning has broken. Occasionally, a guard or two will stop before their shift and buy a cup of house blend and a maple walnut scone before crossing the street and checking in at the staff entrance with its triple-paned, bulletproof glass. Sometimes the guards will set down their cup to retrieve their badge and keys, a slight violation of protocol, but one overlooked by everyone at the jail, especially other members of the correction officers' union.

Within the confines of the small jail, in a not-so-cramped cell, Don Karlsson sits looking at the ceiling, noting a long crack that runs through the concrete. He's wearing blue prison scrubs, with a number on the front and Linn County Corrections printed in large letters on the back. His back is ramrod straight even as he sits on the edge of the bed.

There was a time I swore I'd die before I'd end up here. But things change. Time passes, and you realize the days behind are many and the days ahead are few. You ask yourself, what's the difference if there's less of them? In the scheme of things, addin' or takin' a few away don't matter much, especially when weighed against things that live longer than a man. If I don't step outside in the morning, don't feel the wind, or the rain, or the sun, it ain't gonna matter much. In my mind, I know those things. Even in a concrete box, they're all still there. And the reasons I'm in that box will swirl outside, living on, for what's gonna feel like forever.

A guard knocks on the cell door. "Your lawyer is here."

Don slowly rises and stands. He pushes his hands through a small receptacle and waits for the cuffs before pulling them back. The door opens, and he looks down at the guard, who is nearly a foot shorter with twice the girth.

Once the cuffs are on, Don steps back and the steel bars clank open. He follows the guard down the concrete hall to a small room with a wooden table and two folding chairs. Stacy is sitting in one of the folding chairs, legs crossed while holding a manila folder, her black leather briefcase sitting upright on the floor next to her.

As Don enters the room, she stands. Her face softens, and her eyes well. She hugs Don, much to the consternation of the guard, who clears his throat before stepping out.

Stay away from drugs and the law. That's what I taught the kids when they was young. Nothing good ever comed from gettin' wrapped up in either. But they never listened. And here we are in a jail with its big metal bars and concrete walls. It's all impressive, meant to sober the poor souls whose fate sent them here. And I look around and realize I'm the one who should have followed the advice.

Stacy steps back, takes a breath, and her face regains the seriousness of a criminal defense attorney. She folds her arms.

"Dad, what the hell happened?"

"Things got a little mixed up, that's all."

"You were charged with starting a riot. The sheriff is in the hospital."

Don's face remains stoic. "Billy's friends showed up to help. Might have been a little intimidating for folks."

Stacy sits in one of the chairs and he sits across from her. "What sort of 'friends' were these?" she asks.

"The kind that come along to look for a fight. Men so afflicted by the righteousness of their cause, no words of warning, no misgivings of purpose, no naysaying are within their measure of tolerance."

Stacy raises an eyebrow. "Afflicted by righteousness? Dad, have you started going to church again?"

Don doesn't respond. "Billy's friends were tryin' to scare off the trespassers."

"Were they actually trespassing?"

"Not sure. I didn't see what happened."

Stacy pulls a yellow legal pad from her briefcase and leans back in her chair. "Did you tell anyone to start fighting? Give anyone the idea they should fire a gun or throw a rock?"

Don shakes his head. "Nope."

"Well, that's something." She scrawls something. "What about Billy? What was he doing?"

"Nothin'. He was with me."

Stacy taps her pen on the paper. "Did you yell, or say anything that might have provoked them?"

"Not a word."

She purses her lips and continues tapping. "If you didn't do anything, this should be easy. The sheriff getting injured is probably the reason you were charged."

"Yeah, I figured. Heck, I liked the sheriff. Was doin' a fairly good job as far as I was concerned."

Strange thing, how the man you respect, who's trying to help you, who seems to have it all under control is the one who gets hurt. Like jumpin' in a dog fight, the poor soul that decides to break it up, he's the one who gets bit.

Stacy makes a few more notes before putting the pad back in the briefcase. "We'll get you out of this. The day of the arraignment, most likely."

Don looks at her. "You think this is all much about nothin'."

"What do you mean?"

"Me stayin' on my land. Fightin' for it."

"Dad, we've been over this. Do I want you living out in the middle of nowhere forever? No, I do not. But it's your decision. And until you are legally prevented from doing so, I will try to help you. There may be a point where it's past my ability, and you'll have to move. But until then, I will advocate for you."

"You mean you'll do my lawyerin'."

"Yes, Dad, I'll do your lawyering."

Don leans back in the folding chair. "Ain't none of this what I thought it would be."

"What do you mean?"

"Never thought I'd need you all helpin' me."

Stacy hides a smirk. "Well, there you are. We are trying to help, even Zeke. But in different ways."

THE LINN COUNTY COURTHOUSE is a dozen blocks from the corrections facility. Unlike the jail, which was built in the 1980s, the courthouse reflects early twentieth century Romanesque architecture. Faux white columns blend with long arched windows all in white, unpunctured by color. While the building's appearance may have been intended to elicit gravity and awe, it is both bland and unpleasant to the eye.

The insides of the building, including the courtrooms, are little better. Lined with wood, the rooms resemble the interior of a cigar box, without any of the grandeur or authority that one might expect from a state's seat of justice.

Despite its appearance, the courthouse is remarkably functional. Prisoners enter one area, attorneys another, court watchers another.

When Stacy sees the courthouse, she is reminded of her

years at the University of Oregon's School of Law and how she felt both out of place and unimpressed by the facility and by the implementation of law occurring within its walls.

As she moves through the metal detectors at the front entrance, a young man in an ill-fitting suit waves and quickly walks over.

"Hi, I'm James. The district attorney would like to speak to you."

Stacy glances over but keeps walking. "Unless she sent you with a summons, I'll be in Courtroom Three."

Speechless, he scurries away.

Stacy enters the courtroom. The largest in the courthouse, its maple pews are packed with reporters and interested onlookers. She steps through the bar and sits at the defendant's table. A wry smile crosses her face as she notices the empty plaintiff's table.

After a few minutes, James enters the courtroom, looking flustered. "District Attorney Hayes really wants to speak to you," he tells her.

Stacy nods. "I'm sure she does." She pulls a legal pad out of her briefcase. "James, I want you to give a message to District Attorney Hayes." She scribbles a note on the pad and rips it off. "Take this to her. And tell her I'm going to obliterate her. In front of all these people. Let her know for me." She folds the note and sticks it in his hand. "Thank you, James."

Speechless once again, James turns and walks out of the courtroom.

Soon, a sheriff's deputy escorts Don into the courtroom. Her father is still wearing dark blue scrubs and remains handcuffed until the deputy motions to take them off. Slowly, Don sits down next to Stacy.

She pats his arm and whispers, "The DA is terrified."

Don doesn't move.

A door opens, and a bailiff enters, followed by the judge—

a portly, bespeckled, middle-aged man. Everyone stands. The judge sits without looking up. As the rest of the observers sit, the bailiff announces the docket. "State vs. Karlsson." After a moment of silence, the judge raises his head and looks at the plaintiff's table. "Where is Ms. Hayes?"

Stacy stands. "Stacy Karlsson for the defense. Your honor, since the People aren't here, I assume they've chosen to drop the case."

The judge leans back in his chair. "Would you like to move for a dismissal?"

As Stacy starts to respond, the doors at the back of the courtroom open, and a harried-looking woman enters. She is tall and slender, in a blue skirt and white blouse. Reading glasses are perched atop her head. She quickly makes her way through the bar, followed by James.

"I'm so sorry, Your Honor. I was hoping to dispense of this matter without wasting the court's time."

The judge raises his eyebrows. "It's too late for that, Ms. Hayes. I was about to dismiss the case."

She stands behind the plaintiff's table. "Your honor, the People move to reduce the charge from inciting a riot to killing an endangered species."

Stacy spreads her arms. "Your Honor, that's ridiculous. For starters, killing an endangered species has a greater penalty. It's a federal offense. Unless I'm mistaken, this isn't a federal courthouse." She turns to look at District Attorney Hayes. "What endangered species is my client charged with killing?"

Hayes ignores the question. "Your honor, a sheriff's deputy ended up in the hospital because of this riot. Pretending it didn't happen only means it will happen again."

The judge rubs the bridge of his nose. "While I understand the people's frustration, there needs to be an offense committed in order to charge the defendant. The question of venue raised by Ms. Karlsson is relevant as well. Unless the People have something they can meaningfully support, I'm forced to support the motion Ms. Karlsson was about to make."

Hayes is quiet. Stacy can tell she doesn't know what to do.

The judge raps his gavel. "Very well. Case dismissed."

THE GREEN TORTOISE is unusually quiet for a Friday night. Instead of a rally, small groups of activists are huddled around tables, sipping pints of beer and quietly discussing the events of the past week.

Sally Ramirez shuffles between tables collecting glasses, refilling pitchers, and trying to avoid looking too interested in the conversations. To most of the patrons, she is little more than an attractive Latina taking orders and bussing tables. She makes sure to smile and repeat the details of each order as her black, shoulder-length hair drapes forward, brushing the pad on which she scribbles. She appears friendly, warm, and aloof, as though her primary mission is to ensure each order is correctly filled. She speaks with a slight accent, trying to sound like her grandmother. In any other venue, her speech couldn't be distinguished from her friends, all upper middle-class and white, and would be described by linguists as "general American" with no difference between "cot" and "caught."

Sally understands prejudice. She is aware the people in the room see her as an ally in their cause. They have conflated her ethnicity with their perceived understanding of the Latino population. But they don't know Sally. Sally's brother is a detective in the San Francisco Police Department. Her father was a police officer, and her grandfather was a *policía* in Juarez, Mexico, before local corruption forced his immigration to California. Sally grew up believing the police were always on the right side of the law. When a friend of her brother's asked to help monitor the local activist community, Sally didn't merely agree to help; she immersed herself in the opportunity. Which is why Sally, with her cheerful smile and occasional stumbling over a word, listens intently to everything. Every conversation and every detail.

On this night, she listens to a discussion at a small table in the back of the bar, where two women and three men sip on IPAs and talk about how they will do "whatever it takes" to stop the destruction. She recognizes a reference to the Karlsson homestead and to Donald Karlsson.

"The feds couldn't take him out."

"Someone has to."

Sally sets down her tray, which pauses the conversation. "Qué? Two Full Sails, a cider, and a glass of rosé. Yes?" She passes out the drinks.

"Thank you."

She picks up the tray, turns to leave, but sets it down again and begins to clean the next table although it's already clean.

"Well, who's going to do it?"

"Maybe the bitch daughter will turn on him."

"I heard she's getting the restraining order thrown out."

Sally drapes the towel on her arm and picks up the tray. She walks to the bar and then turns and goes back to the same table.

"It will have to be him. He's the only one. There isn't anyone else who can stop it."

The conversation stops again. "We're out of the Full Sail. Can I get you something else?" She pulls out her order pad.

"How about two Fat Tires?"

Sally smiles. "Sí. Two Fat Tires." She writes on her pad and slowly turns back toward the table. She pauses as the conversation resumes.

"Do you think Zeke can do it? Will he do it? He's the only one who can shut the thing down for good."

Sally walks past the bar into the kitchen, pulls a phone from her pocket, and begins to text rapidly.

. . .

Billy and Don are standing on the porch of the little house when Stacy parks her car in the drive. Don calls the dogs, who diligently sit at his feet.

Stacy walks up holding a blue envelope. "We got it."

Billy crosses his arms. "What?"

"The ruling." She steps onto the porch.

Don looks at the envelope. "That's it?"

Stacy holds it up. "Want to know what it says?"

Billy looks at Don, who is quiet. "Well, yeah."

"Just give us the bottom line," Don says.

Her smile doesn't wane. "It says you can harvest your trees, unequivocally. At least for now."

Billy's face scrunches up. "What do you mean, 'at least for now'?"

"The government will likely appeal, at which point, the appellate court will issue a similar injunction. We'll file a petition to have it lifted based on undue hardship, then they'll argue 'irreparable harm' if the injunction doesn't stand. All of which will force the court to address the injunction and request for relief."

Don sighs. "Sounds like we didn't win, only bought ourselves some time."

"It's better than that, Dad. We won the first round, which is always the most important round. There is going to be more, but this sets us up." Stacy looks at both men. "Dad, you won."

Billy turns, opens the door, and walks into the house.

Don pats her on the shoulder. "Thank you for all you're doin'." He follows Billy inside.

Stacy stands alone on the porch, holding the envelope. She remembers showing her nearly perfect report cards to her father, the similar pat on the shoulder, a meaningless acknowledgment of her success, and the empty feeling that follows. She grits her teeth and marches after Don and Billy.

Billy is standing next to the refrigerator holding a beer. Don is leaning on the kitchen table.

Stacy puts her hands on her hips. "What exactly do you guys think happened? We won. That was the goal. We won."

Billy takes a swig of beer and wipes his mouth. "I figured the court would rule and that would be it. Didn't think that would only be the start."

Don scoffs. "It's how the dagburned government gets you. They wear you down. Think if they push long and hard enough, you'll give up. That's how it works."

"We can always throw in the towel," Stacy says. "I can try and cut a deal."

Billy shakes his head. "That ain't right. I don't want the feds taking this place away. No, sir. We fight on."

Don looks at Stacy. "What do you think?"

"It would be easiest to sell," she says. "You could find somebody with deep pockets who wants the land and has the resources to fight the feds. You'd need to move, but you'd have enough money to find a nice place."

Billy shakes his head again. "Ain't no way we don't fight this. It's about our rights. Dad isn't going to let anyone come in and take away his land."

Stacy sighs. She pulls out a chair and sits. "I have a feeling this is about more than rights."

Billy slams his beer bottle down on the counter. "What are you implying?"

Stacy leans forward. "That you don't care about Dad's rights as much as you care about inheriting this place."

"That's bullshit! I care about this place because it's Dad's home, and Mom is buried here. It's our *home*. Or maybe you forgot!"

Don stands up, eyes gleaming. "Enough! This isn't about

what either of you want. It's my decision. I planted those trees, I rebuilt this house, I raised both of you. Stacy's right. I should sell this place and move away. Might be the smart thing to do. I'll be dead and gone before I get to cut another tree down. And until then, I'm gonna be plagued by tree huggers and lawyers. I ain't got enough time left for that."

"Dad." Stacy leans toward him.

Don closes his eyes then opens them. "But I ain't gonna do that. I know it ain't smart, but I'm gonna fight. Too much of myself is wrapped up in this place to walk away." He points at the countertop where Billy's beer sits. "I put that in when you were two or three, so you could reach up and grab your dinner if I didn't make it home in time. No one who buys this place is gonna know that."

Stacy straightens. "What are you gonna do when you can't take care of it anymore? When you can't harvest your trees to pay the tax, or clear the brush away from the drive, or fall and can't get help? What then?"

Don's face softens. "I take it one day at a time. I may not be able to make it out here forever, but I'm not lookin' to leave yet. But if I have to leave, I will."

Billy picks up his beer. "You aren't going anywhere."

Stacy nods. "All right. We fight on. For now. But at some point, I need to go back to Boston, and you're going to need a long-term plan." She looks at Billy. "You need a plan."

He nods.

Don crosses his arms over his chest. "Before we get to fightin' the feds, I think there's gonna be more trouble."

"If protesters show up again," she says, "you two need to be less confrontational. The DA won't be as lenient a second time."

"I don't want them on the property," Don says.

"That's fine, but you need to let the police handle it. If you do something stupid, they'll use that against you in court." She looks at Billy. "That includes you."

Billy rolls his eyes. "Maybe if they come up here, we'll just start knocking some trees down."

Stacy shakes her head. "That is not a good idea."

"But it's legal to cut, isn't it—at least, for right now?"

"Technically, yes. But being provocative isn't smart. You need to think of the big picture. If you want to win, keep a level head."

Don looks at Billy. "Not to worry. Billy will mind his manners. Won't you?"

He takes a swig of his beer. "Yeah, sure. But I think having some deterrence will help."

"What do you mean by 'deterrence'? If it's like the last time, I'd suggest you consider something else."

Don raps his fist on the counter. "We'll put up a fence for starters. Barbed wire. Something on the property line."

"There is no way those people will respect a fence," Billy says.

Stacy nods. "The fence is a good idea. But Billy's right—it won't keep everyone away, but it'll help."

"If they cross the property line," Billy says, "we need to send a message. They lost in court, and that don't give them the right to trespass."

Stacy looks at him. "If you're thinking of bringing your redneck friends back, you make damned sure they stay away from the crowd."

"And no guns." Don's eyes gleam with intensity. "No guns."

Sheriff Jensen doesn't take time off. He finds it unbecoming for the head of a law enforcement agency to step away from the job, even for a short period of time. Which explains his bad mood when he returns to the office only a week after he was hospitalized with a concussion.

The flowers someone has placed on his desk don't help. Neither does the card from Miriam Walters, who sits on the County Board after running on her support for the sheriff's office. Miriam has no experience in law enforcement, but with the perceived political benefits of being associated, she wrangled and arm-twisted her way to become Jensen's "partner" in managing the office.

Jensen sits at his gray metal desk and pulls a file from the stack piled on top—a collection of all the collars that rise to felony status before they go to the DA. He flips through the file quickly, makes a few notes, and puts it in another pile that will eventually be sent across town to the prosecutor's office. This one is a burglary, two car thefts, and a possession with intent to distribute later. He stands up and stretches his back.

Derek Tipman sticks his head through the door.

"Hey, Sheriff. Glad to see you're up walkin' around."

Jensen grunts. "How long did Don Karlsson spend in jail?"

"Few days, at least. Charges were dropped."

"Goddamn it. Who was the prosecutor?"

"Marcy Hayes."

"Well, no wonder. They couldn't find someone competent to try him?"

Tipman shakes his head. "Nope. She was the only one who'd even take it."

Jensen grimaces.

Tipman smiles. "Well, like I said, glad you're back."

"Thanks." Jensen turns back to his desk and opens the first file as Detective Betty Hargrove steps through the door.

"Hey, Sheriff. Good to see you."

Jensen doesn't look up. "Why does everyone keep saying that? Yeah. What've you got for me?"

Hargrove crosses her arms. "Might have a little intel on the next protest up at the Karlsson ranch."

Jensen's eyes widen. "Really?"

"Yup. Informant said she overheard some of the activists talking about getting rid of the old man."

"Who are the activists?"

"Not sure. Group that meets at one of them sports bars."

Jensen's brow furrows. "That doesn't help much. We don't know who the likely perpetrators are—"

"Well, maybe we do. The same activists said it was going to be his son."

"Billy?"

"No. Zeke."

Jensen turns and looks out the rectangular window. He has a third-story view of the department's carpool, filled with a mix of marked and unmarked cruisers and the occasional Blazer. It's a view that quiets his mind and helps him think.

"What do we know about Zeke?"

Hargrove closes the door. "Not much. Graduated from high school, did a few years at University of Washington, moved to Eugene, and worked at the Lang's Nursery for several years. Never married. No criminal record. We have an address, but we're not sure if it's current."

"Is he affiliated with any of the environmental groups?"

"Probably, but we haven't pinned anything down."

Jensen turns to face Hargrove. "Well, we should probably find out."

"Yes, sir. How do you want us to do that?"

"Best way I know how. I'll go have a chat with him." He picks up his hat and steps toward the door. "And call that preacher. See if he can go talk to the old man. If jail didn't work, maybe a little God-fearing will settle things down."

. . .

Pastor Rich's Pontiac wagon slowly rolls up the Aegolius Highway. As the road nears its end, he turns down the Karlsson driveway, careful to avoid the large rocks placed in the middle of the drive. He slows when he sees the "No Trespassing" signs flanking both sides.

Technically, the Aegolius Community Church doesn't belong to a specific denomination. While clearly Protestant, it isn't affiliated with any of the Presbyterian, Methodist, or Lutheran hierarchies, nor does it clearly fit within the traditions of any of the modern, evangelical movements. At best, it might be described as loosely Baptist, owing to the baptismal ritual undertaken once or twice a year in one of the deepest waterholes in Aegolius Creek. The timing of these events is critical. Too early in the spring, and the current will be strong and the water muddy. Too late, and the waterhole won't be deep enough to adequately immerse the congregant.

Pastors at the church are paid a small salary and given shelter in the rectory, a small cottage next to the church. They come from a variety of different orders and are chosen by the Church board primarily based on their willingness to come.

The church itself is a simple affair, with little more than a tiny narthex, a pulpit, and a choir riser overlooking the nave and pews. The single steeple rises from the entrance and at one time likely had enclosed a bell, though no one can remember exactly when the church might have had—or, for that matter needed—an actual bell. Its exterior and interior are painted with a reverent gray, an industrial paint donated by Lew's Truck and Trailer in Brownsville.

Within the physical structure of the church, it is the large room below the nave—the basement—which is most relevant to the community, both as a seat of religious fellowship and community organization. Here, on its linoleum-covered floors, countless potlucks, prayer breakfasts, fundraisers, and even political rallies have been managed. Members of the community flock here in times of crisis, in moments of celebration, and whenever the highly individualistic and somewhat reclusive residents of the Aegolius Valley require a safe place for social interaction. In this space, refuge is sought during troubled times.

Pastor Rich is in his mid-sixties and suffers from diabetes and gout. He prays regularly for relief, both from his medical conditions and for better health insurance, neither of which God has granted since his prayer began. He is a well padded fellow, jovial in both word and countenance. Despite his background in a large evangelical Baptist church, he has embraced the more secular routines afforded by his role in the community. He oversees Halloween parties for children who, due to the logistics of their homes, cannot trick-or-treat like children in towns and cities. He mediates disputes between members of the water board. He attends to those who are near death, whether church members or not. And so on.

It is in this spirit, outside of his traditional ecumenical duties, that Pastor Rich has agreed to meet with Donald Karlsson after being asked by someone from the Linn County Sheriff's Office.

As the Pontiac approaches the house, Rich rolls down his window to make sure Don can see his face as he arrives. He parks the car and waits for the dogs to approach, barking and yelping, before he opens the door to get out. Slow and nonthreatening. Just here for a talk.

The minute I saw that car roll up, I knew it was a preacher. After spending years sittin' in the pews, I can spot a preacher a mile away. They dress simple, drive a simple car, approach you pious like.

The door to the little house opens, and Don Karlsson steps onto the porch. He's in a white tee shirt and well-worn jeans. He yells, and the dogs run back to the porch. His chiseled face shows no emotion as the preacher approaches.

"Hello, Don. My name's Pastor Rich. I'm the minister at

the Aegolius Community Church. I heard about what happened here and wanted to come out to make sure you were okay."

Don doesn't move. "I'm fine."

Pastor Rich moves closer. "Great. That's just great. Some of the folks in my congregation were worried, so I said I'd check on you after the riot."

First thing they do is try and put you at ease. Get your guard down.

"If anyone was worried, they'd come out and see for themselves. Wasn't much of riot."

Pastor Rich nods. "Of course. But folks weren't sure how they'd be received, given the injunction and all."

Now you get to the reason. Which ain't ever really the reason.

"People around here know I ain't got a problem with them. I disagree with some about all kinds of stuff, but everything is neighborly. And family matters more than anything." Don cocks his head to one side. "I get that folks were worried about the brawl. I know the sheriff was real mad."

Pastor Rich is quiet briefly before he responds. "Sherriff Jensen's a little concerned is all. He doesn't live up here and doesn't know you too well. He thought I might be able to help."

"You tell him I'm fine, and there ain't no problem with him comin' out here. Sorry you had to drive all this way."

Pastor Rich's brow furrows. He isn't getting the responses he expected. "Yes, of course I'll tell him. I sincerely hope, you know, that given everything that's happened, there isn't a problem."

"There ain't."

He clears his throat. "Look, Mr. Karlsson. Don. Can I call you Don? Look, Don, I'll level with you. Everyone I talk to is worried you might cut down some more trees and get sent back to prison. They don't want any more trouble."

And there it is. The real why-are-you-here question answered. 'Bout time.

Don slowly nods, his back straightening so that he reaches his full height. "I see. Well, to be honest, I'm not sure what I'm gonna do. Government's all tied up in knots. I might cut some more trees, and then, I might not."

Pastor Rich nods. "I see. You know, when I have a dilemma like this, I always ask myself, what would God want me to do? I'm curious, Don, what would God want you to do?"

"I mean no offense, but I don't know, and I'm not sure I care. God seems to take away pretty much everything he gives, so I ain't sure doin' what God wants is really gonna matter much."

Pastor Rich takes a slight step back.

I can tell the preacher don't like my answer. I see him strugglin' to figure out how to respond. He looks at me funny. God weren't there when Marle died. And I didn't see him helpin' much with the kids.

It takes a minute for Pastor Rich to figure out what to say next. After an awkward moment passes, he says, "I read in the paper you planted all these trees."

"Almost all of 'em."

Pastor Rich points up at the canopy overhead. "They're beautiful. I think God has blessed you."

"Maybe. But it may also be a whole lot of work and toil that went into them. I didn't see God out there cuttin' back the vines and scarin' off the deer. That stand of trees grew 'cause I gave it everything it needed to grow. And the squirrels and the owls and even the daggum voles live in them trees. Because I grew them."

A breeze winds through the upper branches of the canopy. Pastor Rich takes a deep breath. "I understand. You feel you should be able to do whatever you'd like with them. But I want you to know there are people who love and support you who are worried something will happen if you do any more logging." He sticks out his hand.

Don shakes it. "I'll consider it. And thanks for coming out."

Pastor Rich smiles. "Will you pray with me?"

That's always how it ends with a preacher. They want to pray. Like God's up there listenin' to all the preachers talkin' about stuff that God ain't got nothin' to do with. Not that I mind prayin'. Seems a little wasteful. And God don't show up when you need him anyway, probably 'cause he's busy, or it's all part of a plan you ain't privy to. The thing the preacher never tells you is just how invisible we are to God. In the scheme of things, we ain't nothin' really. Nothin' important, anyway. Way God probably sees it, we're like stones at the bottom of the creek, sittin' under the water slowly sinking into the muck, out of sight as the current sweeps past us. He's barely aware we exist.

THE APARTMENTS at Fourth and Taylor have seen better days. Their light brown facade has decayed to a dirty white. Moss has festered within cracks in the parking lot. The numbers over the entryway door are readable only by postmen and firefighters. Yet, like so many buildings in the heart of Eugene, a certain, fleeting dignity emanates from its visage. Perhaps it's the faux oil lamps affixed on each side of the front door, or the patterned carpeting in the foyer, or the bronze call buttons on the panel near the door. Whatever it is, the old apartment building exudes a sense of aged, regal decadence, rather than cheap housing for graduate students at the university.

Jensen has seen the building from the street but has never paused to look beyond its faded, exterior walls. After all, how many graduate students become part of the criminal element? He parks the unmarked police cruiser across the street and assesses whether to enter or wait. He is alone, purposefully, and doesn't want to incur any sort of hesitancy beyond that of a friendly law enforcement officer stopping by for a chat. It's his forte, the friendly chat, and he gives it great weight when deciding exactly how to approach a potential perpetrator.

Jensen exits his car and walks toward the front door. He waits a moment on the street until he sees a young couple walking out deep in conversation. They exit, and as the door slowly closes, he lunges toward the handle.

But Jensen misjudges the distance, and the door closes a moment before he reaches it. He sighs. Twenty years ago, he'd have been quick enough to grab the handle. Frustrated, he reaches down and yanks until miraculously, it opens. He makes a mental note to tell the owner to start locking their front door.

The lobby of the building has a musty smell. A pair of elevators next to the entrance look like they were installed in the 1950s, with rounded, chrome-plated doors and a dial-shaped floor indicator.

Jensen makes his way to the second floor and finds room 231. He looks up and down the hall. All's quiet. He knocks.

For a few moments, nothing. He knocks again. Still nothing. As he turns to leave, he hears feet shuffling inside the apartment and decides to wait.

A voice calls from inside. "Just a minute." More shuffling is followed by the click of a deadbolt and the turning of the handle.

The door opens, and a half-awake Zeke steps out. He's wearing a gray sweatshirt and cotton pants. On his left forearm is a tattoo of a trillium flower. His shoulder-length, dirty-blond hair is tangled. Jensen assumes he's been asleep.

"Zeke Karlsson?"

"Yes."

"I'm Sheriff Rod Jensen. I've got a few questions for you if you have a minute."

Jensen is surprised when Zeke motions for him to come inside the apartment. He expected a harsh welcome. He wonders for a moment if he has the right guy.

The apartment is small and minimally furnished. There is a loveseat, a table, and a few chairs. Above the couch is a large painting of Marys Peak and the Willamette River. Books are stacked on the carpet.

Zeke motions for Jensen to sit at the table. "Want some coffee?"

"No, thanks. I apologize for dropping in on you so unexpectedly." Jensen looks at one of the paintings. "Is that Mount Spencer there?"

Zeke nods as he sits across from his visitor. "No problem. What can I do for you?"

"Well, it's like this. After the incident at your father's homestead last week, we've been listening to different groups in the community."

"You mean spying?"

Jensen smiles. "We listen to what people say publicly, like everyone else. No cloak and dagger stuff." He leans forward. "In some of those public conversations, we heard you and your father disagree about whether he should log his trees."

Jensen likes making direct statements, not so much to elicit honest reactions, but to gauge responses. He uses the same strategy when he plays poker with some of his deputies on Thursday nights, puts his cards face up on the table after every hand. The responses reveal intent. Knowing a person's intent is the key to understanding what they are going to do.

"Yes. That's correct," Zeke says.

Jensen doubles down. "They say you don't think he has the right to log."

"It's not whether he can; it's about whether he should."

"What do you mean?"

Zeke puts his hands on the table. "What matters is there's a species living in those trees, which may or may not have been there from the beginning of time. They're part of that ecosystem and part of the larger ecosystem of which we are all a part. Destroying them isn't in anyone's interest."

"But if it's your father's land—he owns it, after all—why shouldn't he be able to take from it whatever he wants?"

"Is it really his land? Do we ever really *own* land? I mean who owned it before Dad? The federal government. And before that? The British, or maybe the Russians. And before them? The Calapooia? The Chemapho? Or maybe the Peya? And who owned it before them?"

Jensen tries again. "Will you try to stop him?"

Zeke sits back in his chair. "I'll try to convince him."

"And if you can't?"

A slight smile crosses Zeke's face. Jensen can't decide if it's evidence of intent——or if it indicates incredulousness at the question. It doesn't give him a sense of what Zeke has planned.

"I'll do what I can to prevent my father from destroying the habitat of an endangered species, no matter how much he cares about his damn trees"

Jensen nods. "And how far would you go to stop him?"

"You think I'd hurt him?"

"It's just a question."

Zeke's face becomes appreciably more serious. "I love my father and would never hurt him. But I do intend to stop him if he continues down this road." He pauses. "And I think you should leave."

Jensen slowly stands. "Well, thank you for your time. I think you've answered all my questions." He always says this last part to leave the impression their unsaid responses have revealed much more than intended. If there is to be a crime, best to let the potential perpetrator know ahead of time that you're onto them.

As he makes his way back to his car, Jensen notes the meticulously manicured flower beds surrounding the apartment complex. A distant penchant for gardening, before his back and knees started to hurt, has left him acutely aware of well-placed plants. A combination of rhododendrons, fuchsias, and azaleas are arranged in a semicircular ring, with the larger plants set closer to the building. At first glance, the plants appear rooted, as though they've been cultivated within the soil where they sit. On closer inspection, Jensen can see they sit in small pots, covered by mulch, and aren't connected to the earth around the apartment complex at all.

THE BAR at the Hilton Hotel in Eugene hasn't been updated in nearly thirty years. Once a hub for out-of-towners headed to a university football game or a show at the Hult Center, it has seen better days. The yellow-brown carpet and faux maple finish behind the bar have long since lost their allure. But like all establishments that face little competitive pressure, the management hasn't seen fit to update the bland decor better suited for a different time when a Hilton was considered a high-end accommodation.

Stacy sits alone in a booth, a stack of accordion files piled up next to her. Amid the papers on the table sits a Manhattan with rye, up, barely touched. Her flats are off, a pair of readers perched on top of her head.

Jerry steps into the bar, trying to remember the last time he'd been here. Was it to meet his boss about a federal murder trial appeal? Or perhaps an out-of-town Ninth Circuit judge whose signature he needed for a warrant? Was it a decade ago? More? He looks tired, befitting his recent courtroom loss. No briefcase in hand, only his phone with a cryptic message.

Jerry sees Stacy and approaches the booth. She sees him but doesn't look up. He clears his throat. "If I knew Storr and Kraus were sending their franchise player, I would've asked for help. Congrats on your win."

She looks up and smiles. "Didn't think I'd be here either."

She motions for Jerry to sit. "How do you like getting your ass kicked?"

Years working at the DOJ in Washington have left Jerry with an ability to avoid flustering and keep a poker face even when confronted. He smiles. "Like I said, had I known…"

Stacy nods, appreciative of his professionalism. She sensed it in the courtroom but needed to see it in person to be sure.

He looks around. "Not sure how my boss would feel if he saw me here."

"The case is closed. And he's my father, not a client."

He smiles again. "Fair enough."

Stacy sets down her pen. "We need to settle this thing."

"I think the judgment was clear. You won. 'The claimant's petition is granted,' if I recall the precise wording."

Her smile fades. "For now. But my father is old. Old and implacable. He's afraid of leaving. And this will come up again. And again. I know the drill. And he can keep fighting it, but—"

"I get it. But that day hasn't come yet. What exactly are you asking me to do?"

"Consider an appeal. And ask that the injunction stand until the appeal has a chance to be processed."

Jerry frowns. He still isn't sure why he's at this meeting. "Counselor, I'm a little uncomfortable discussing what your client needs when it appears to be in direct contradiction to what he *says* he wants."

Stacy puts both elbows on the table and stares at him. "Jerry, are you suggesting I've not advocated for my father as aggressively as I should?"

"No, no, nothing of the sort."

"Good. I'm only trying to do what's best for my dad." She leans back into the cushions in the booth. "All I'm saying is that it's highly likely my father will violate the injunction, and if he does, he can be removed from the premises. And that wouldn't be a bad thing for him. I'm telling you this so you can be ready. Ready for him to do something he shouldn't." She pauses for a moment to let Jerry absorb the humanity of her position. When he doesn't respond, she continues. "And I think something terrible is going to happen."

Jerry shakes his head. "What?"

Stacy looks away. "I don't know. Were you here when the mill shut down?"

"No."

"It was bad, so much upheaval. People who thought they had a future suddenly didn't. They looked around and wanted to turn the whole world on its head."

Jerry sits with the information for a moment, reassessing the motivations of his opposition. He thinks about how to respond. And for the first time in as long as he remembers, he cannot find the words.

CHAPTER NINE

"Whoever's is the soil, it is theirs all the way to Heaven and all the way to Hell."

— *THE AD COELUM DOCTRINE*

Up West Burnside Street in Portland, where it turns from a street into a road, there is a stainless-steel medallion embedded in a concrete platform. It marks the place where a small, concrete obelisk once overlooked the Tualatin Valley. From that spot, one can see out to Oregon's wine country, a region rich with a mixture of soils and rainfall titrated in a perfected alchemy to ensure that grapes, particularly pinot noir, can be grown, harvested, crushed, and fermented into wines to rival the best in Europe. Weekend visitors to the area wend their way along country roads, through the rolling hills from vineyard to vineyard, slowly becoming inebriated as they taste the bounty of the land. None have any inclination to stop and look at the obelisk or its replacement marker, to wonder who put it there, or to consider why it's engraved with the word BASE-

LINE on one side and the more auspicious WIL and MER on the other.

The obelisk was placed on June 4, 1851, only a year after Congress established the office of the Surveyor General and created a Federal Court and Land Office in Oregon City to mark the intersection of two lines, one connecting the Pacific Ocean to the Snake River, and the other connecting the Columbia River to California. Shortly after it was placed, land surveyors began working their way across Oregon Territory, starting at the obelisk, cutting the land into 640-acre pieces.

Surveying land in Oregon wasn't as easy as in the Midwest or along the Eastern Seaboard. The land was rugged, with mountains and rivers, the deep gorge through which the Columbia River poured, and the sharp foothills at the edges of the Cascade Mountains and dense temperate rainforests on the coast. It took over a year to reach Oregon City, only a few dozen or so miles from the obelisk. It would take nearly three decades before the remainder of the state, or at least the inhabited areas, were measured.

Survey work was complex and hard, and often less precise than might be envisioned by those versed in cartography. Areas in which boundaries were disputed could be scrutinized, but frequently, regions less accessible were left alone. Fieldwork included not merely measurements of distance and altitude, but notes about waterways, vegetation, and specific landmarks that a cartographer might use to create an official map.

When the first surveyors made their way up the Aegolius, they took careful notes about rock formations, ridgelines, and the passage of the creek. As it was, they came in late summer, long after the spring runoff had ended, and the waters had receded to a modest trickle. They took several weeks to collect data-making notes, all of which the mapmakers in Oregon City would use to fill in blank sections of the nascent state.

In addition to collecting data, the surveyors placed markers, cast iron metal disks affixed to concrete atop metal pipes sunk deep into the soil. The disks are small, a few inches in diameter, unimposing, inscribed with the mark of the United States Geological Survey and land section numbers. Like the brands affixed to livestock, the markers are used to assign ownership and order, symbolic and pragmatic measures of size and distance.

Today, on occasion, children of the Aegolius will stumble across one of the survey markers and wonder what it represents. They will question why someone affixed a smooth, round piece of metal to the earth, and what the inscription "USGS" means. They will wonder if it means something, or if it matters. But as the moment passes, the little discs, civilizing marks on the untamed wild, evidence of the artifactual presence of man's order fleetingly stamped on nature, will seem of little consequence, and the children will return to their play.

THE TIN CAN Rooster Cafe and Bar rises from the Willamette Valley floor like the head of a beer drawn too fast from the tap. It's seen better days. The yellow-painted siding is bubbled and cracked in places, and the shingles on the roof are covered with moss. The parking lot is more mud than gravel, the glass door in front covered in dust enough to be mistaken for a giant piece of cardboard. The linoleum floor gets washed once a month. To see the checkerboard pattern beneath layers of spilled beer, the mop must go over it twice.

At the bar, an abundance of cheap alcohol, from Stetson whiskey to Rusky's vodka is lined in bottles of various shapes and sizes. There is beer on tap, though not a recognizable brand anyone cares to imbibe. Cases of Henry's are stacked beneath the bar, along with a few six-packs of Schlitz, and some thirty-two-ounce bottles of malt liquor.

The Tin Can's patronage is predominantly male,

composed of farmers, bikers, truck drivers, and the newly unemployed. Unlike most bars, it's busier during the week and when social security checks get cashed than it is on weekends or during a sporting event. Men come directly from work, if they are employed, or during the day if they are not. Whenever they arrive, they are there for one singular and clear purpose—to drown the depressing trajectory of their lives in the ferment of grain. To forget and never remember. To go somewhere and matter, if only for a few hours.

Late in the evening, Billy steps up to the bar, orders a Henry's, and takes a seat at a small table, where Tom sits with a whiskey, straight up. Tom is relaxed, and Billy can tell this isn't his first drink.

"I hear your old man's lookin' for some protection."

Billy nods. "Yup. He's pretty freaked out by all the tree huggers."

"Any idea when they'll be back?"

"Well, the court order got thrown out, so it's only a matter of time."

Tom takes a sip. "Love to put a cap in some of them libs."

Billy smiles. "Send all them snowflakes runnin'."

"For argument's sake, let's say I could round up a few guys to help protect your dad's property. Would he have any problem if they were armed?"

"Naw, Don don't have a problem with guns. He still hunts, I think."

"And if one of the boys thinks they did have to take a shot at one of 'em?"

Billy takes a deep breath. "They'd be protecting his land. Don't get me wrong, I'm sure he doesn't want to see anyone get hurt unless it's necessary."

Tom nods. "Of course." He takes another sip of whiskey. "I know some Second Amendment types. True believers who want to bring back local control of public lands, that sort of thing. I'm sure if I put out the call, a few of 'em would show up."

"Dad would appreciate that."

"Couple of 'em are still fighting charges from that Malheur thing, so they might stay away on account of outstanding warrants. But we'll have enough."

Billy looks back toward the bar. "Good. I don't want to start any trouble, but let's make damn sure my dad gets the protection he needs."

As they talk, three men enter The Tin Can. They sport leather and camo, jeans and steel-toed boots. All three are bearded. One has a holstered gun hanging from his belt.

Billy stands as the men approach, and they shake hands as Tom makes introductions. "These are some of the folks I was talking about. Constitutional defenders. They can help us out."

The men pull up chairs as Tom waves at the bartender for more beer.

The largest of the men, burly and serious, addresses Billy. "We've heard about your problems with the federal government."

He nods. "It's been a mess."

"We understand. Motherfuckers in Washington think they know what's best. But it's always the little guy who gets hurt. We've fought these battles before, and if you're willing, we'll be there to defend you and yours as well."

Billy taps the table, not certain whether his willingness matters.

Tom clears his throat. "We believe in every man's right to do what he wants with his land."

One of the other men interjects. "We're part of the Citizens for Constitutional Freedom, Oregon chapter. Patriots fighting against the tyranny of the federal government."

Billy takes a swig from his beer. "I appreciate your willingness to help. The government arrested my father for cutting down a tree he planted himself. My sister's a lawyer and got him out of jail, but we think at some point, they're going to take control of his house and the property around it."

Tom puts his hands on the table. "Don, that's Billy's dad, is older and not capable of fighting them off. He's lived on that land for sixty years. It don't seem right."

The men nod in agreement as the beers arrive.

"Tell your old man we've got his back. When they come—and mark my words, they will come—we'll be there to provide resistance."

Billy scratches his chin. "I appreciate that. But I have to ask—what's in it for you?"

One of the men smiles. "If they come for one, they come for all. First, they take your father's property, then soon enough, they come take mine. If we can make them think twice about what they're doing to your dad, they might think twice about coming after us."

"How will you guys resist?"

The largest man responds. "We will assert our Second Amendment rights."

Billy looks at Tom, who doesn't say anything.

"You okay with that?"

Billy raises his beer. "Hell, yes."

A SMALL GROUP of vehicles surrounds the old Wigwam burner in Brownsville. The rusted structure is only one of several buildings on the site where the Willamette Sawmill Company was once headquartered. The mill was torn down years ago, and the administrative buildings are hollowed-out shells with tan, brick facades and broken windows. The burner is two-and-a-half stories tall, a cone of metal with a mesh top. For decades, millworkers shoveled slash, trim, and sawdust onto a conveyor belt at its base, then watched as the discarded bits of wood fell through a hole near the apex of the cone just below the mesh. Back in the days of the mill's operations, smoke rose from the giant furnace all day and night. At night light from the burner would flicker a dull orange, illuminating the other buildings and piles of logs, occasionally emanating from flames rising through the mesh, reaching up from their container of steel.

Next to the burner, Zeke stands, arms folded, with a thoughtful look on his face. Around him, a dozen men and women hold their breath. They are here to ask Zeke the question, the one they've debated since an idea was hatched after their last meeting at the Green Tortoise. The question they'd dreaded asking but felt compelled to ask. Now, with the question hovering in the air, they await his response.

Zeke puts his hand on the rusted metal. "I'm not opposed to confrontation, but I'm just not sure how effective it will be."

A woman with a brown ponytail, wearing a flannel shirt and Gore-Tex Keens, smiles. "We aren't asking you because we think it will be confrontational. We're asking because we think it will make everyone reconsider doing anything rash. You're family. That raises the bar for everyone involved."

Zeke takes his hand off the rusted metal and stares at his palm. He rubs his hands together. "I'm not sure this kind of protest will work. It lasts as long as people are willing to stay, and no one can stay indefinitely. My dad can just wait them out."

A man with a green tee shirt and graying hair clears his throat. "The hope is that he sees his son trying to stop him, he'll back down. It seems like our best chance. At the end of the day, if he really wants to log his trees, he's going to log them. But maybe we can get his attention and help him rethink things."

Zeke half-smiles. "You don't know my dad. It's hard to

convince him of anything." He touches the side of the burner again.

A few people nod. The woman with the ponytail steps forward and pats Zeke's arm. "It's a brave thing you're signing up to do," she says quietly.

Zeke doesn't respond. He stares at the top of the burner. "You know what happened to these things?"

No one responds.

"They passed a law. Little communities in rural areas had enough of the smoke, so the state decided to phase them out. Happened without any fanfare and barely a mention in the news. When a certain number of people want something, it happens. It's quiet. It's fast. The longer and slower something takes, the fewer people support it. I'm not sure if this is going to speed up or slow down the removal of those trees."

"Are you saying you don't want to do it?"

Zeke looks directly at the man. "What I'm saying is before we do this, we have to ask ourselves the fundamental question any protester should ask—Am I hurting or helping the cause?"

The man blinks, unsure how to respond.

Zeke isn't certain the man grasps what he is asking. He looks around him, wondering whether anyone understands how many people they can affect. He is certain they don't. And then he realizes the decision is his. The weight of idealistic hubris and humanistic determinism are his to sort out. The faces around him are vacuous, the faces of people who don't come from the forests. People who've never held a chainsaw up against the soft bark of a cedar or shoved a seedling into the ground with a hazel hoe. But here it is. The decision, which in the end is his alone. He knows what he thinks, what he's tempted to do. Walking away wouldn't solve anything, only bury the inevitable seeds of revolt, anger, and angst. Like weeds in cultivated soil, they would grow unfettered.

He clears his throat. "I think on balance, doing this is

better than not. It's a tough call. And if we are wrong, you and me and everyone here will need to accept that we didn't make things better. I'll do this, but only because I decided there was a little more good than bad in taking action. But in the end, I really don't know. None of you should pretend that you do, either."

The men and women waiting for Zeke's answer think for a moment. Collectively, they expected to breathe a sigh of relief or disappointment. Instead, they climb into their cars sullen, grave, and uncertain, ready to push forward, but shaken by newfound ambiguity.

Three pickups and a brown sedan slowly rumble down the Karlsson drive. The pickups are all several years old. At least one has a gun rack visible in the back of the cab. The car is an older Camaro, mostly restored, with bright chrome finishings and an inauspicious Confederate flag bumper sticker.

The vehicles stop in the graveled area before the little house. Seven men emerge and take notice of the surroundings. It's a warm summer day, and light filters down through the canopy onto the driveway and the house. A light mist has dissipated and left sparkles of dew on the plants and trees.

Two barking black labs bolt around the corner. The men are unfazed, even as the dogs growl and menace.

Don Karlsson steps through the front door and onto the porch. His white tee shirt is punctuated by red suspenders affixed to frayed jeans. His Redwing boots are laced up tight. He yells at the dogs, who immediately quiet and wag their tails.

The men, one of whom is wearing a visible sidearm, approaches the porch. The leader, tall and broad-shouldered with a handlebar mustache, is wearing a Dickies jacket and black flannel shirt. He sticks out his hand. "Don Karlsson, I'm Mike. Nice to finally meet you."

Karlsson shakes his hand.

"We've been in touch with Billy. He's worried the government's comin' after your land. We're here to help defend it."

"Not sure I need defending. I got a lawyer for that."

Mike's gaze is steady. "Well, we've had some experience with this. If the government wants something bad enough, they'll come get it." The other men nod in agreement.

Don appears unmoved, even as he agrees. "S'pose so. And what do you fellas do to stop the government?"

A man in the back responds, "We lean on the Second Amendment."

Don doesn't say anything.

"We simply make certain no one trespasses without an enforceable warrant," Mike says.

Don seems to be considering whether or not he wants this kind of enforcement. Mike and the men shift uncomfortably as they wait for him to speak. Each man feels Don's penetrating gaze and for a moment, their bravado peels away.

"You all can stick around and help keep order." Don looks directly at Mike. "But I don't want no shootin'. Carryin' is fine if it helps maintain order. But no shootin'. I hear a shot fired and the next one'll be my twelve-gauge."

Next to Mike, one of the men speaks. "Someone comes up on me, I will defend myself."

"You shoot at someone on my property," Don says, "and you'd damn well better have a good reason. And comin' up on you ain't one. Hell, you all came up on me. You think I ought to come out here spoutin' buckshot?"

Mike raises a hand. "I think Jim means if we're under attack and need to defend ourselves. Doesn't mean we're going to shoot because someone steps in our direction."

Don looks carefully at Mike. He sees a pudgy man in his mid-fifties, with thinning salt-and-pepper hair, a stupid mustache, and an arm sleeved with tattoos. He has a hardened appearance—or more precisely—the look of someone trying to appear hardened.

He nods. "All right. You can help. But no shootin' Whatever happens, no shootin.'"

A SMALL GROUP of vehicles pulls off the Aegolius Highway onto a dirt road not far from the Karlsson homestead. It's early evening, and the August sun is beginning to touch the tops of the surrounding hills. The air is soft and warm. A breeze chases its tail along the length of the valley. Station wagons, vans, and a couple small pickups line the edges of the road. As the passengers exit vehicles, they carry ropes, two-by-fours, pulleys, hammers, and other tools. They are mostly young, twenty and thirty-somethings. They move quickly and quietly toward the Karlsson ranch driveway.

A few yards up the driveway, they stop amid a group of large trees, barely out of sight of the little house. A large, black lab saunters down the driveway and barks only once before it's quickly handed a small bowl of hamburger and given friendly pats on the head.

Once within the grove of Douglas firs on the homestead, they surround a large tree not far from the highway. A pair of young men don climbing spurs and harnesses. They extend ropes along both sides of the tree and slowly begin to ascend, working their way up through the branches. Three stories up, where the trunk is only about eighteen inches in diameter, they attach a flip line to a pulley and drop a rope to the ground. A bucket is attached to the rope and pulled up by the climbers. Dropped again, a two-by-four is tied and brought up by the climbers. Then another.

With agility and speed, the climbers begin to attach pieces of wood to the tree. A small frame is built around the trunk of the tree, with braces anchored by attachment bolts. Finally, pieces of plywood make their way up the tree trunk, and one is fixed to the frame. When completed, a small platform has been created, no more than five feet wide and six feet long, with the trunk of the tree running through its middle.

Throughout the process, the group has been silent, using only hand signals to communicate. As the climbers descend, the rest pick up their tools. Then, as quietly as they've come, the group departs, leaving only the platform, barely visible to anyone who might be standing below.

CHAPTER TEN

"And the Lord said unto Cain, Where is Abel thy brother? And he said, I know not: Am I my brother's keeper?"

— *GENESIS 4:9*

The summers in western Oregon are as glorious as a cotton candy sunset chased by sprinkles from the Milky Way. The days are hot, and the nights cool until mid-August, when temperatures reach their zenith, and heat rises from the asphalt highways, and trees absorb the sunlight until they begin to bake and harden like bacon that's been on the griddle for too long.

But the beauty of the season is tinged with a dread that maligns the joy felt by residents of the Aegolius. During the summer, when families descend on Buckshot Park to sprawl on the carefully cut, green grass, and Aegolius Creek is still swollen enough, kids can wade in chest-deep while adults glance at each other every time someone mentions the heat. Pleasantries about the beautiful setting or the warmth are packed with the unspoken language of shared fear. They know within the lazy days of summer are the dangers of a wayward spark from a metal grinder falling on a bed of dry needles, a discarded cigarette butt thrown in the grass on the side of the road, or an exploded transformer on a powerline showering sparks into the brush; these common, simple acts can turn the browning green into a raging inferno.

It wasn't always such. While fires have ravaged the forests since the time of Adam, century-long rises in temperature and forest management plans to maximize timber production—followed by a near cessation of removing anything from the forest—has left a tinderbox, ready to explode. The forest is full of fuel, doused with the accelerant of excessive heat.

And the people of the Aegolius know. They hide their anxieties in coded language and wait with bated breath. Like people sitting on a mound of dynamite, they wait. Even as the Aegolius revels in the late summer, one can hear sighs of relief whenever the fall rain finally begins.

For the first time in as long as he can remember, Hamfort doesn't know what to do with his truck. Called to the Karlsson homestead to carry a load to the mill, he tries to make his way onto the drive but is stopped by a blockade of humanity squarely positioned in the middle of it. His initial instinct is to simply keep driving; he is in a large, slow-moving truck, after all. It seems rational that the protestors would move as the vehicle rolls toward them. But a more thoughtful examination leads Hamfort to think otherwise.

Aside from the protesters standing before him, he sees a group of large rocks—small boulders, really—situated in the drive. The rocks themselves aren't particularly imposing; they could easily be pushed aside by the truck's bumper. But some of the more ardent demonstrators have seen fit to chain themselves to the stones. The sheer audacity of people chaining themselves to rocks in the drive gives Hamfort pause. He's used to moving timber from the forest to the mills. He isn't confrontational.

So Hamfort has stopped. Stopped right between the five-foot-tall posts on either side of the Karlsson drive. He sits in the cab, unsure what to do next. The protesters haven't touched the truck and look like the crowd at his daughter's softball game. The heat is sweltering.

KENT DRIVES his old Subaru up the Aegolius toward the Karlsson homestead. It isn't the first logging protest he's covered, and he's learned to approach cautiously. As he gets closer to the Karlsson drive, he notes the cars lining both sides of the highway—a mixture of Subarus, small pickups, Audis, BMWs, and old Volkswagens adorned with bumper stickers.

A three-string, barbed wire fence has been erected around the edge of the property. Kent can tell it's new. There are posts on either side of the entrance where a gate might hang, complete with hinges, but no gate. A log truck sits idle at the entrance. A small crowd of thirty or forty people, stand in front of the truck chanting something Kent can't make out. The driver, a middle-aged, chubby fellow with a baseball cap sitting in the cab, appears exasperated.

As he moves closer to the open gate, Kent notes that the small crowd on both sides of the fence has placed several large rocks, not quite boulders, on the gravel driveway. A few protesters have chained themselves to the rocks. Further up the drive, he sees plastic tarps wrapped around the base of several large trees close to the driveway entrance.

Kent parks on the side of the road, gets out, and steps past the log truck, through the gate, and onto the property. He skirts the crowd and makes his way further down the drive, looking for Don Karlsson. As he approaches the small house, he sees a clutch of vehicles, a combination of four-by-fours and motorcycles. Several men are standing in a circle talking, a few clearly armed. He considers approaching them but is reticent. His journalistic instincts suggest observation is the best approach to reporting on whatever is going to happen at the Karlsson homestead.

Sheriff Jensen makes his way to the center of the crowd. He gauges from the general mood that this isn't like the last protest, where he could find folks with whom he could reason. Not that things turned out well when he did, but at least it had started off calm. The group today seems more assertive. He shakes his head at a couple of protesters who've chained themselves to rocks next to the drive. A small backhoe could pick the rocks up and move them, protester and all.

Jensen waves Trent Ridge and two other deputies toward the crowd surrounding a log truck blocking the gate. He notices a handful of protesters around the base of a large tree twenty or thirty yards beyond the Karlsson fence. He approaches one of the older men there. "You've got to move back to the property line."

The man looks at him with disdain. "As soon as you protect the forest."

Jensen nods. He understands what this means: a long afternoon of arrests. Backbreaking work, even by police standards. It's one thing to cuff a person, especially if they aren't violent; it's another to have to carry them back to the cruiser. He waves at Trent and points at his wrists. Trent nods and walks toward the Blazer. He'll bring back enough zip ties to hogtie the entire bunch.

As Trent moves to retrieve the zip ties, Jensen heads back toward the truck. On some level, he's glad it's there. A physical barrier to entering the property isn't a bad thing. Still, he needs the protesters to move. He waves at the driver, who rolls down his window. Jensen pulls himself up near the cab. "I'm gonna try and get these folks to move, but I can't have you assisting in any tree removal today. I'll get 'em out, but you can't be hauling, either, or I'll have to arrest you as well."

The driver, looking exasperated, smiles and nods. "Sure thing, Sheriff. I only want these clowns to leave me alone."

Jensen gingerly steps off the truck and hops to the ground. He makes his way to the dozen or so people standing in front and waves his hands to get them to quiet down. "Listen up! You are all welcome to protest, but you can't do it on private land. You are trespassing. I need you to move outside the fence."

Several people boo, and a woman raises her middle finger as Jensen points toward the gate. He steps behind them and begins to shoo them toward the fence. No one moves. Jensen sighs. He resigns himself to more zip ties and a sore back.

KENT RETREATS to the highway and notes the small crowd has grown from a few dozen to nearly a hundred. The log truck driver is still sitting in his vehicle, which remains stuck at the gate. He sees the flashing lights of the sheriff's vehicles, a Suburban and two cruisers parked in the middle of the highway. The sheriff and several deputies are huddled talking.

After a few minutes, the deputies walk toward the crowd, step inside the fence, and attempt to herd them back outside the fence. Many comply but those chained to the rocks remain, as does a small group huddled at the base of the largest tree. Two of the deputies approach those around the tree and begin to converse. The deputies have a handful of zip ties and are holding them up in front of the protesters. Kent tries to move closer so he can hear the conversation, but the crowd is chanting.

As Kent watches, one of the deputies begins to push two of

the protesters standing near the tree back toward the road. One pushes back and both deputies immediately wrestle him to the ground and tie his hands behind him. As they do, one of the protesters yells at the deputy and points to the top of the tree. For the first time Kent notices the ropes dangling from high up in the canopy.

Don Karlsson stands on the porch with his hands on his hips. Billy and several men are in front of the house, and he can hear chanting voices down the drive. The protesters are back. He hoped Hamfort could have made it to the house, but he called Billy to say he's stuck at the gate.

The men standing near Billy are agitated. Don made it clear that firearms are not acceptable, but some of them are packing anyway. He knows the sheriff is likely to be in attendance and another untoward event won't bode well.

A short, balding man with a large belly looks at Billy. "Can't believe how many dirt worshipers showed up."

Billy nods. "Goddamned lot of 'em."

Don, wanting to get an idea how many 'goddamned dirt worshipers' really are in attendance, marches down the drive. Billy and the rest of the men follow. A few hundred yards from the house, he sees Hamfort's truck and the crowd surrounding it. He stops and stares. He can make out the flashing lights of the police cruiser.

One of the men points up in the canopy. "What the hell is that?"

A series of ropes hangs from one of the trees. Don wonders why anyone would put ropes up one of his trees.

Billy's face darkens. "That ain't right. We can't use that Doug fir, but they can? No, sir. Not today."

A couple of the men nod.

Billy storms off, back toward the house.

I know they're comin'. Whole bunch of cars filled with longhairs. I know Zeke's with 'em. On the one hand, the boy is pushing against his old man, and it ain't right. But then, I'm kinda proud of him, too. My son, leadin' the charge, even if it's against me. Something about seeing the child as a man makes you proud.

Billy stands on the porch next to Tom with a look of righteous indignation. "What the fuck do they think they're doing!" He sees the protesters standing around the base of a tree. Tom yells something, and a handful of his men run toward the group screaming and shouting. The protesters fall back to the highway.

Don stands next to Billy. "What's that?" He points to the upper branches of a tree where the protesters had been standing. The branches shake and move.

Tom pulls binoculars out of a bag. "Someone's climbing up there. Goddamn it! Sonofabitch is gonna get to that platform." He turns toward Billy. "You want us to put some buckshot in his ass?"

Before Billy can reply, Don interjects. "No guns! I thought I made that clear! No guns!"

Tom puts his binoculars on the porch railing. "All right. It's your property. We can just wait 'em out."

There ain't no way I'm gonna have someone shootin' guns round the house. When the kids was little, I taught 'em 'bout guns. Don't point 'em unless you're gonna shoot. Don't shoot at water 'cause the bullet ricochets. Don't shoot at somethin' unless you see all of it. Some yahoo pulls a trigger and who knows what's gonna happen, where that bullet's gonna go.

Billy grimaces. "They're tree sitting. Goddamned infestation. There's a platform, and one of them is making their way up. We don't need guns to take care of this." He turns and walks back into the house.

Never understood why someone sits in a tree to keep from cuttin' it down. Don't do nothin' for the tree next to it. Don't stop someone from takin' down the rest of the forest.

Billy steps out of the little house with a chainsaw in his right hand. "The court said we can cut trees, so by God, let's cut some trees."

I ask myself why someone wants to trespass. Trespass is a kind of stealin'. When someone trespasses, he's takin' away someone's security, and feelings of safety and privacy. It feels like the worst kind of stealin', cause there ain't no hope of getting what's been stolen back. You lose what's been takin' with no hope you'll ever see it again.

STANDING BY THE BLAZER, Jensen radios for more help. At least another four or five deputies are needed, particularly if the crowd resists. He sees Trent digging through equipment in the back of the vehicle, looking for more zip ties, when he hears the sound. Jensen has heard enough chainsaws to recognize the roar. He sighs again. Karlsson has decided to be provocative. More zip ties.

DON FOLLOWS as Billy marches down the drive, waves of visceral anger emanating from his every step. The handful of Tom's men flanking him are decked out in American flags, "From my cold, dead hands" tee shirts, baseball caps, and a black Stetson. One lets forth a pugilistic "Fuck the tree huggers!"

It's out of hand, I tell him. The crowd is out of hand. The hippies sittin' in the trees, they'll come down soon enough. Just wait 'em out, I says. But Billy ain't to be stopped. Ain't goin' to be prevented from doin' what he's goin' to do. He got the Stihl in one hand and a wedge in the other. And the crowd's cheerin' him on.

AS THE DEPUTIES drag another zip-tied protester back toward the highway, Kent sees the men who had been standing around the house moving down the drive toward the protests. At least a half dozen, some with sidearms, two with rifles, and Billy with the blade of a chainsaw balanced on his shoulder are marching toward the protest. Billy has a scowl on his face. A few of the protesters notice and start to point. As more become aware, several begin to move back toward the highway. The two chained to the rocks suddenly look terrified, and those near the great tree put up their hands and begin to retreat.

Billy approaches a tree and pulls the chainsaw's starter cord. As it roars to life, he begins a cut at the base. Two of the protesters scream and yell, pointing at the ropes in the canopy. The men can't hear the protesters over the sound of the chainsaw.

One protester begins to run toward Billy but stops cold when a man pulls out a pistol and points it directly at her. Kent can see several protesters screaming at Sheriff Jensen.

JENSEN NOTICES PROTESTERS running toward him. They look panicked. They yell and point at the tree, but he can't hear them over the sound of the chainsaw. He waves his hands, and a woman stands before him, screaming above the roar of the saw. Initially, Jensen can't understand. Then, in a flash of clarity, he realizes what's happening. He rushes back toward the log truck, the crowd, and the large tree.

AS THE SAW digs deeper into the wood, the tree groans. Kent watches as Billy steps back, and the undercut he has made yawns open. The men with guns and the protesters gasp as they hear a loud crack, and the tree begins its fall. The branches whistle through the air and a woman screams, still pointing toward the platform near the top, visible as the tree begins its descent.

. . .

Jensen makes his way past the log truck when he hears the loud creak and groan of the tree as it begins to come down. It's parallel to the highway, which he briefly considers a fortunate fact since it won't fall on the crowd.

As the giant tree descends, the branches whistle through the air. It appears to fall slowly, though with immense power. Jensen makes out a small platform with someone attached to it, descending along with the tree. The giant Doug fir lands with a thud and bounces before settling on the ground. Jensen runs toward the platform, which shattered on impact. A body is attached to it, face down and unmoving. He sees the tattoo of a flower on the left forearm. It's Zeke.

Kent looks back at Billy. A moment after the tree falls, Billy drops the saw, the zeal of vengeance replaced by a look of uncertainty and then concern as blood rushes from his face, and he follows Jensen.

As Kent approaches the shattered platform, he pushes his way past a few of the protesters. For the first time, he sees Zeke's body, lifeless, cradled between two large branches. There is a bit of blood around his mouth and nose. Don Karlsson and Sheriff Jensen are kneeling. Billy is holding Zeke's arm, and Don has his hand on Zeke's chest. Jensen has his hat off as he talks into his radio.

Billy pats Zeke's face. He slides to his knees next to Don. "Zeke, you're gonna be okay. See, I'm here, Zeke. Just like when we was kids. I'm here. You're gonna be okay." He shakes his brother's chest as though he's trying to wake him, then shakes harder. His voice rises in the still-settling air. "Zeke. Wake up, Zeke. It's Billy. I didn't know it was you, Zeke. I didn't know it was you…"

Two deputies push past Kent with a first aid kit. Clumsily, they open the kit, pull out the AED, try to discern where to put the pads. They roll Zeke's body over.

THE CROWD SCREAMS when the tree falls, until a man in a Stetson points to the arm. It grows quiet. The crowd parts as Don pushes his way through to the front. He sees the arm. His shoulders slump, and his face drops. He kneels and puts his hand on Zeke. Someone in the crowd says, "Got what's comin'," and in a single motion, Don rises and cracks his fist across the nose of the source before turning back toward Zeke.

I SEE THE ARM. It's got the outline of a white, three-petaled flower right there, above the elbow. I think for a moment there's lot of folks with flower tattoos. No way it's Zeke's arm. Not his. Not here. Not his arm.

But I know. I know whose arm it is and how it got there. That's Marle's favorite flower he's got tattooed on, one she'd seen when she first come home with me. Said it meant three little ones was comin'. And I feel like when the nurse came and told me Marle was gone. Only this was worse. It's both Zeke and the little bit of Marle that's left, that shard of her buried somewhere inside him. Both are gone. I see the arm, and I know it. Know it the minute I see it.

CHAPTER ELEVEN

"Thou shouldst not have been old till thou hadst been wise."

— *KING LEAR*, WILLIAM SHAKESPEARE

THERE WAS a time when the Aegolius, like many rivers and streams that run into the Willamette River, would fill with silver ribbons of fish. In the autumn of each year, the chinook and coho would fight against the current, navigate increasingly shallow riverbeds, and circumvent the array of predators seeking an easy meal. Even as the Aegolius shrank from a river to a creek, the salmon would come.

In places where the creek was shallow, the fish could be seen undulating back and forth, writhing their way through the water and muck to places where the water ran clean and cold, freshly melted from the winter snowpack. By the time most reached their destination, the lower portion of their bodies were torn and ragged. Millions of years of evolutionary drive pressed the silvery fish onward and upward, further and further from the ocean toward their place of reproduction and death.

Local tribes regarded the returning fish as a gift and took

the opportunity to take as many as they could smoke from the creeks. Early European settlers did the same. Though already flush with game, each year the fall came with this added abundance.

By the time Donald Karlsson made his way up the Aegolius, the salmon run had vanished. The United States Corp of Engineers erected a series of dams along the tributaries of the Willamette, hoping to minimize flooding of the valley's fertile farmland. The giant, concrete barriers dried out the riverbeds, and predatory birds proved too much for the fish, who finally succumbed.

Today, there are few fish in the Aegolius. A few, wayward trout, confusing the Aegolius with the McKenzie or Santiam, are the only glints of silver on the bottom of the creek bed. Those sandy patches, which previously cradled salmon eggs, sit empty.

In recent years, the dams that once harnessed and restricted the flow of the Willamette are on the verge of removal, and the river waters may soon flow from the snow-pack to the ocean unimpeded. Yet even with the return of the river flow, the salmon may not return. Fleeting is the hope that the Aegolius will once again bristle with the fins of salmon, returning to a place that was their nursery and graveyard. As time passes, the plausibility of the salmon's return has faded.

But thinning hope is not extinguished hope. One wonders if the progeny of the salmon that once occupied the Aegolius basin aren't imbued with the same instinctual sense of place, honed over millions of years, that drove their ancestors up toward the headwaters. Perhaps one day a single salmon, a prodigal child, will find itself lost in strangely familiar waters, climb the Aegolius stream bed, lay its eggs in the murky sand, and return the species to its rightful home.

. . .

STACY MAKES her way to the Linn County Hospital in a haze. She briefly recalls her last time to the hospital, when Billy broke his arm in the eighth grade. At the time, it was a gray cinder block building with a red and white "Emergency" sign perched at one end. She remembers the tiny waiting room with a large desk manned by a single nurse wearing light purple scrubs and a dark-blue name tag. There was a pair of vending machines filled with soda and snacks. She wonders for a moment if they were there when she saw her mother for the last time.

Stacy notes a police cruiser and Sheriff Jensen's Blazer parked in the tiny lot next to the Emergency sign, which appears unchanged. She marches into the waiting room where she sees a nurse in blue scrubs standing at a desk. A handful of people sit in plastic chairs throughout the waiting area. All appear somber.

The nurse looks up as Stacy approaches. "Can I help you?"

"I'm here to see Zeke Karlsson."

"Are you family?"

"His sister."

"One moment." She disappears through the glass doors and returns a second later, motioning for Stacy to follow.

The Linn County Hospital Emergency Room has a total of six patient bays separated by curtains, surrounding a U-shaped desk where two nurses and a physician are seated. Sheriff Jensen and a deputy lean over one of the desks talking with a nurse.

As they enter, the nurse turns to Stacy. "Before we go in, you need to know this may be disturbing. I want to make sure you are prepared."

"I've seen lots of dead bodies. I'll be fine."

The nurse looks surprised and turns back toward the center of the room.

As if on cue, a physician sitting behind the desk stands and steps toward Stacy. "I'm Dr. Lewis." He shakes her hand. "I'm so sorry. Your father and brother are here." He leads her to one of the bays and pulls back the curtain. Zeke is covered by a sheet, except for his shoulders and head. His eyes are almost closed. Stacy finds this odd; the bodies she has seen in the past all had their eyes open.

Billy is leaning over Zeke, his eyes red and wet. Don sits in a chair next to the gurney, his shoulders slumped and face sullen.

Stacy feels her knees weaken before she can steel herself. She steps between Don and Zeke and puts a hand on both. She closes her eyes and tries to imagine Zeke as a child, the little towhead crawling through the moss and ferns, picking up a toadstool here, a clover there, every bit as alive as the flora and fauna around him.

"What happened?"

Billy shakes his head, his mouth quivering. "It got out of hand. It just got out of hand."

Don doesn't speak.

Stacy stands for several minutes without speaking. Finally, she steps out of the bay and finds Jensen.

"What happened?"

Jensen clears his throat. "Stacy, I'm real sorry for your loss."

"What happened?"

"Billy cut down a tree. Zeke was on a platform up there."

"What?"

"I need to ask you, and I don't mean any disrespect, but was there any animosity between Zeke and Billy? Any fighting? Arguments?"

Stacy points a shaky finger at Jensen. "You know this was a fucking accident. There isn't any way Billy would ever hurt Zeke."

Jensen nods. "You know I have to take Billy in."

"You've talked to the DA?"

"I didn't have to. He reached out, told me to arrest Billy."

"For?"

"Murder one."

Stacy shakes her head. "It's an election year, isn't it?"

Jensen nods.

"Have you told Billy or Dad yet?"

"Not yet. I'm giving them some time."

She looks at the draped bay holding Zeke's body. "I'll talk to them."

"Take your time. We'll go get some coffee."

Stacy heads back to the curtained bay and bows her head for a moment before pulling back the curtain. Don and Billy haven't moved. She puts her hand on the gurney and takes a deep breath. "Billy, I know you didn't mean to do this, but the DA is going to charge you."

He doesn't look up. He strokes Zeke's hand.

Don looks at Stacy. "He didn't do it on purpose."

"It doesn't matter. The DA's still gonna charge him."

Billy stands. "He's right. I did this." He pats Zeke on the arm and exits through the curtain. Stacy follows. Sheriff Jensen and his deputy are standing at one end of the Emergency Room, near a set of sliding doors that lead to the ambulance bay. There is a yellow light over the doors that blinks every few minutes. The light bounces off the glass behind Jensen, silhouetting his frame. For a moment, Stacy thinks she might be looking into the gates of hell.

As Jensen's deputy takes Billy into custody, Don emerges from behind the curtain. For the first time in her life, Stacy sees an old man, hunched forward, broken in half.

I REMEMBER one winter when the rains came hard, and the creek got all swollen. There was this doe and her two fawns crossing the creek, which was deep and runnin' fast. Something happened on the far side of the creek, and the doe turns and starts back. One of the fawns goes with her. The other tries, but it can't get all the way turned around before the torrent of water knocks it off its feet and pulls it under. I sat and watched, waiting for it to pull its head up, pull itself up on a rock or kick over to one bank or the other. Maybe there's a ledge or an eddy or some such thing where it goes down. Whatever it was, the fawn that got pulled under never surfaced, never stuck its head out of the water, never managed to make it to the shore. And the doe had to sit there and watch, waiting, wondering what ever happened to the fawn that was supposed to be behind her.

After a time she nudges her remaining offspring and wanders away, leaving the creek, unable to scream or cry or throw herself into the current. She leaves as though nothing has happened. But I know she leaves bearing sadness and guilt. She leaves with a burden that will never lift, will never recede, a cloud forever upon her soul.

RAIN BEARS DOWN on the little house. It's late summer rain, the kind that isn't supposed to happen until the rainy season has started in earnest. The storm is out of place, in the way a rare event can puncture the regularity of the natural world. The rain comes in waves, torrential for a time, then slow and steady. It rolls off the corrugated overhang above the porch, and the leaves and moss covering it are so bloated with moisture, the water seeps into little streams lining the grooves of roofing and pours off the edges like a dozen waterfalls to the muddy ground below.

The F-150 rolls up the gravel drive toward the little house nestled at the base of the giant grove of trees. The dogs bark incessantly as it stops. Rob steps out of the driver's side and ignores the dogs as he marches toward the front porch. Before he can set foot on it, the door opens, and Don Karlsson steps out.

Don looks imposing. The crevices in his face mirror those

of the surrounding hills, carved from solid granite. For a moment, Rob looks with awe, as though a giant has stepped from within the tiny abode. Never mind that Don has a shotgun under his arm.

Rob takes a step back. He nods toward Don in a manner that only someone in rural Oregon would, to acknowledge the presence of the shotgun. But Don doesn't nod in response. Rob knows this means the shotgun is loaded.

"Donald Karlsson?"

No response.

"My name is Rob." He points to the passenger in the truck. "That there's Harvey White."

Without a word, he holds up an envelope. "This is an offer. For the back ninety you've got growing over there."

They finally come. Come to take it all. Not with guns. With briefcases full of lies.

Don doesn't move. Rob wonders if he's about to feel a barrel full of shot.

"They ain't for sale."

Harvey gets out of the truck. He holds a raincoat over his head as he steps up next to Rob. "So we've heard. Still, we'd like to extend an offer." He nods toward the envelope. "I think you'll find it quite generous."

They come like the Pharisees. Come to give Judas his bag of silver. But Judas don't take it at first. No sir. He considers his options, thinks maybe there's a way out.

Rob clears his throat. "Look, we know you can't log. I'm sure it's quite frustrating. We can help. We can buy your land. I know the taxes and such aren't goin' away. You'll still have to pay. And without your trees, that's going to be hard."

Don's face remains unmoved.

"I can see you may need to think about it."

Rob sets the envelope on the railing next to Don.

And there it is. Thirty pieces. Sittin' right next to me. And I got to ask, is this what it's all worth? And that's it, ain't it? When they come to take, they take everything. Everything you are and everything you'll ever be. I look back and only see what was never gonna be again. I look forward and see only pain.

KENT SITS at Starbucks on 13th and Broadway, a handful of blocks from his condo. His laptop is open, and he stares at the screen, not quite sure where to begin. He has only a few hours to finish a final piece about the Karlsson homestead. He hears the loud hiss of milk being frothed and the bland conversation of the people seated at the tables behind him. It all seems trivial, which is why he comes here to write:

"What ties a man to the place he lives? Familiarity? Every day starts the same as the last, and like an old shoe, the place becomes soft and feels good and smooth when it slides on. Or is he molded by the place until all that he is, body and soul, is only made whole when he's at home? Or does a place seed some ethereal spark that reaches into one's personage and infects their imagination and dreams? What is it that sinks deep into the valleys of our mind and makes us remember, taste the rain falling off the leaves of the old maple, feel the ruddy bark of the sapling and smell the cedar that's just been split and stacked behind the barn? And what happens when that place is torn away, skin from muscle and bone, rescinded from present consciousness into the fading smoke of memories? Is it lost? Or are we who were once there?"

Kent looks up. A woman with a small dog in a shoulder bag is trying to order something at the counter, but the dog is clawing to get out and the woman is pushing it back in, keeping it contained.

"Is there a point in preserving it? When it stands a million years and remembers the wagon trains and native sweat lodges and saber-tooth lions and inland seas and dinosaurs, what is the point? It has no memory, no recollection of the brief period in which we said it was ours, when we called it our own."

The dog finally acquiesces to its owner's insistence, and the clerk, somewhat dismayed, types the order into the touchscreen at the counter.

"A second of ethereal spark, is that enough? Being able to call a place 'home.' Is it enough?"

EPILOGUE

"The land shall not be sold in perpetuity, for the land is mine. For you are strangers and sojourners with me."

— *LEVITICUS 25:23*

WHENEVER I LOOK at the aftermath of a forest fire, it seems random. One tree might be completely charred, burned right to the core, every ring turned to charcoal, while the trees next to it are barely singed. A pile of moss might smolder for days, gradually scarring the forest floor, while the sword ferns at its edge lose only a few fronds. But if you look more closely, the randomness begins to make sense. The tree that turned into charcoal may have been an old spruce, filled with sap ready to explode into flames like it had been doused with gasoline. And those next to it were old oaks with thickened bark covered with lichens, which wouldn't burn even if their sap was replaced with lighter fluid. It's the subtle things, carefully crafted by the evolutionary forces that ultimately determine what happens in a fire. On the surface it may appear the cards are randomly dealt. But nothing in the casino is left to chance. Fate, as it were, was predetermined long before the game was ever played.

It took three days to put out all the smoking embers left on the Karlsson homestead. The fire never really had the ability to expand much, owing to the valley's relatively humid conditions. At most, it may have consumed forty or fifty acres surrounding the house, stopping at the roads to the south and east, and the creek to the west. The trees adjacent to the house seemed to bear the worst of it. Most could only be logged for salvage. Those beyond were less affected by the fire.

Even in humid conditions, forest fires usually burn human structures to the ground. Once, Tad offhandedly mentioned to us—and like most of Tad's bits of wisdom it proved to be an immutable fact—human domiciles, caught in a fire, burn totally and completely. Doesn't matter if they are made from wood, brick, or metal. Nothing remains standing when the fire is gone. Nothing. It's as though fire is nature's immune system, provoking a fever, even destroying a few of the body's own cells, all to kill off whatever isn't part of its own. The human germ is exposed and eliminated before it can do damage to the forest body.

With that in mind, it wasn't a surprise that the Karlsson house was totally incinerated. All that remained where it stood was the dark ashen residue of burnt wood and molten metal.

When Donald Karlsson was incinerated, we called everyone for help: the Forest Service, the Crawfordsville Fire Department, even the county sheriff. In a half-hour, a few volunteer firefighters showed up. They didn't even try to get close to the house, which by that point was nearly gone. They shot some water from their truck at what seemed like random spots around the property and then left when the truck ran dry. In the end, we didn't get to old man Karlsson's body until it was little more than a pile of ash; the only human bits left that we could see were a few, jagged teeth.

A medical examiner came a day later, but by that time, the water we'd sprayed on the fire had washed away a good portion of Karlsson's ashes. Still, the ME collected what she could, including the teeth, in a small metal box, took some pictures, and drove away.

After the fire, everyone was spooked. Tad spent the next few days inspecting every inch of the area. I didn't know what he was looking for, but Tamara said Central Command wanted him to investigate, and he was looking for details to put in a report. I asked Tad why they hadn't sent an official arson investigator. He shrugged and mumbled something about clueless idiots in Salem.

I'm not sure what Tad found to report, but there were some oddities about the Karlsson fire that confirmed it was arson. The forest was wet enough that it seemed unlikely anything would burn without the use of an accelerant, and the trees that had burned weren't going to end up completely charred unless an accelerant was applied to each one. Many of the trees burned from the ground up, which is the opposite of trees burning in a naturally spreading forest fire. Whoever started the fire likely placed an accelerant on the base of every tree before setting them alight. Given the hundreds of trees burned, the process itself must have been careful and deliberate.

And, of course, there was Donald Karlsson's self-immolation. The day after the fire, the county sheriff and one of his deputies showed up. They rolled down the driveway in a white Blazer. The sheriff kept shaking his head as he looked over the embers where the house had been. He questioned each of us —Tad, Jose, Tamara, and me—about what we had seen, where we'd been standing when Karlsson was on fire, and whether there was anything he had said or done that might have indicated why he decided to burn himself and everything else.

The sheriff's questions had an effect on the group. Witnessing a man burn to death triggered pent-up fears most of us felt whenever we were out working a line. After the sheriff left, Tamara spent a lot of time sitting in Rudy the truck. Jose stopped eating for a day or two. Both said they were going to do something different next summer.

I WAS TURNING over and dousing a few remaining embers next to the creek bed when I heard her voice. "Can't believe the goddamned creek bed stopped the fire."

I turned and saw a well-dressed woman with dark brown hair pulled into a ponytail. Her jeans were clean, and she wore an REI vest, which looked like it hadn't ever been donned outside. I couldn't tell looking at her whether she was local or from somewhere far away.

"Yup, the creek made a good fire line." I pointed back to the trailer. "Too bad the house wasn't on the other side of it."

She folded her arms over the vest. "I think that was the point." She looked sad, in the way that people who aren't merely sad, but also angry look. "I can't believe the son of a bitch burned it all down."

I cleared my throat. "You mean Mr. Karlsson? You knew him?"

"To the extent anyone ever knew him, yes." She took a few steps into the burnt rubble of the house and moved some of the ashes around with her boot.

"Why'd he do it?" I asked.

She sighed. "Grief. Or anger." She took a step onto the pile of ash where the porch had been. "When people have something taken away, they sometimes destroy everything that's left in the hope that won't be taken away, too."

I looked down at the charred earth, unsure what the appropriate response might be.

She knelt and picked up something small among the ashes. I was going to tell her she shouldn't take anything, but I couldn't think of a reason why not.

AFTER WE'D FINISHED DOUSING everything around the Karlsson fire, we were called back over the mountains to a burn outside LaPine. It was only partially contained, and Central Command was worried that increasing winds would accelerate the spread before it could fully be brought to heel.

I tried to sleep in the bed of the truck as it meandered up the McKenzie highway toward Sisters and Bend, but whenever I closed my eyes, all I saw were smoldering embers and wind-whipped flames surrounding Don Karlsson's frame.

We drove through the lava beds outside of Sisters, where we could see across Oregon's central plain. The snowcapped peaks of Mt. Bachelor, South Sister, and Three Fingered Jack rose up from the central valley floor as though something deep in the earth had sought to pierce the veil of wispy clouds hovering near their peaks. The dark lava bed, laced with bits of obsidian and pumice, flanked the highway above the roadbed for several miles like charred snowbanks. In places, pine or junipers had managed to take root in bits of soil between the mounds of black rock—stubborn remnants of life in the otherworldly landscape.

Outside of Bend, we stopped at a small park at the bottom of a knoll. Tad and Jose sat on a park bench while Tamara and I stretched out on the grass. Since the fire, we avoided talking about what we'd witnessed. We kept ourselves busy. But in the evenings, when we sat around the truck preparing to bed down for the night, a quiet melancholy hung in the air.

Now, with a mountain range separating us from the Aegolius, the veil of silence was ready to be broken. Tamara, her hands behind her head as she looked up at the blue central Oregon sky, began. "How does someone do that?"

Jose took a deep breath. "No idea."

"I remember reading about monks during the Vietnam War setting themselves on fire," I replied, knowing I could no more conceive of how to answer the question than Tamara or Jose.

Tad picked a dandelion out of the grass and stroked it in his hand. "Whatever it was, it must have been terrible." He tossed the dandelion back on the ground. "Terrible and painful. People who harm themselves are usually in pain."

"Yeah, but the idea of burning…" Jose's voice trailed off.

For what seemed like a long while, no one could think of anything else to say. Finally, Tad's phone buzzed, breaking the silence. As he answered the call from Central Command, we all stood slowly and walked back toward the trucks.

As we drove the remaining distance to LaPine, an east wind began to blow. Heat rose from the central valley floor, streaming in waves toward the sky, roiling with a growing number of clouds into a single rising plume. Hazy, black smoke carried by the wind drifted over the pines and junipers before being forced toward the heavens by the heat. Massing together, the clouds and smoke roiled into a giant mass, a wall stretching above the trees to heights beyond the edges of the sky, leaving an eerie orange glow.

I heard the first drops fall into the back of the truck and looked up to feel more on my reddened skin. The scattered drops soon became a torrent. As the rain fell, the dust and soot that had accumulated on everything began to wash away, leaving behind little trails of mud. As the water fell on my face, it mixed with the tears streaming down my cheeks.

IT'S ODD how people think they can own land. That somehow the land, a place, can belong to a person. If anything, it's the other way around. Though we are migrant creatures, capable of traversing every corner of the earth, there is always a place that calls to us, pulls us back, defines who and what we are.

Mrs. Green used to say that God gave the land of Canaan to Abraham, which eventually became Israel. I don't think it was that simple. After all, God had to take the land away from the Canaanites, who were there first. And if history is any guide, it was something of a Faustian bargain. Had Abraham known how many wars would be fought to control that little sliver of land, he might have declined. But he didn't. And his offspring have been fighting over it ever since.

Mr. Lewis, who teaches economics at Crawfordsville High, would say that we value places because of their location or what we can take from them. If that's the case, Abraham got a raw deal. Israel is the only place in the Middle East without oil. The only value of Abraham's strip of land is perception. The existential belief that Israel belongs to one group or another is the only reason anyone would see fit to fight over it.

All of which is to say, we never own land. The land owns us. It ties us to it, binds us in a way that we can never escape. Its hold reaches into the core of our being and wraps itself around who and what we are. When there's a break, when we lose our place, our souls become untethered nomads, wandering in a desert of identity. We become lost in the flames of our own purpose and are never the same again.

ACKNOWLEDGMENTS

Aegolius Creek is dedicated to my parents, who decided to raise me and my siblings in the Mohawk Valley, Oregon, which is the source of much of the content. My father, Larry, is from Powers, Oregon, which could have served as Ken Kesey's Wakanda every bit as much as the Mohawk Valley might be Aegolius Creek. His background as an attorney in the timber industry proved instrumental in helping with the legal and timber industry language–and it would not have been the same without him. My mother, Michele, helped with the initial developmental edits. As an artist, she has encouraged my creativity for most of my life, and I would not have taken up the pen without it.

My writing group, Novelitics, and its leader Kim Taylor Blakemore, have been a constant source of encouragement. Writing is a solitary craft. Being part of a group improves both the product and attitude.

Finally, this book would not have been written without my wife Melissa who suggested it would be therapeutic for me to 1) write and 2) write something about my upbringing. I'm not sure this is what she meant, but it has proven well worth the effort.

There are communities up and down the western slopes of the Cascade Mountains like Aegolius Creek. The effects of the timber wars in the 1980s and 90s left many decimated economically and socially. The people in these places are generally not wealthy nor can they easily change their circumstances. They continue to suffer the long-term impacts today.

As we go through the necessary economic and societal changes to mitigate climate change, it is worth remembering there are those who pay a larger price to save the environment than others. Have compassion for their sacrifice.

ABOUT THE AUTHOR

Micah Thorp is a physician and writer in Portland, Oregon. He grew up in the Mohawk Valley, outside of Springfield, Oregon which serves as a paradigm for the fictional Aegolius Creek. His first novel, *Uncle Joe's Muse*, and its sequel, *Uncle Joe's Senpai*, were published in January 2022 and March 2023, respectively. *Uncle Joe's Muse* won the Next Gen Indie Award for Humor, and Forward Indie Gold Award for Humor. Some of his other literary works have been published in *Cleaver Magazine*, *Fictional Café*, and *Blind Corner*.